I0623001

RETURN TO ME

FARRAH ROCHON

Wandering Road Press

Wandering Road Press, P.O. Box 990 Gramercy, LA 70052

**wandering
road
press**

For the many fans who have read and supported my Holmes Brothers series throughout the years.

Thank you for demanding Jonathan and Ivana's story. I wrote this for you.

Return To Me

Three years after his bride-to-be jilted him at the altar, Jonathan Campbell is still struggling to expunge every reminder of her from his life. His new motto is to never again expose his heart to such anguish. But when she pops up uninvited on his doorstep, his life is suddenly upended all over again.

A case of cold feet sent Ivana Culpepper running the week before her wedding. She found refuge and purpose in Haiti, working with relief aid organization Operation: Heal. When a series of circumstances force her to return to her hometown of New Orleans, Ivana must face the consequences of her actions and the bitter rejection of the man she once loved.

Can Ivana convince Jonathan to give her another chance, or is her betrayal too much for their newly reawakened love to overcome?

Chapter One

THE STIFF BREEZE blowing off the Mississippi River whipped Ivana Culpepper's long, natural hair around her head. She caught it up and twisted it in an attempt to tame the mass of wavy locks, to no avail. Forgetting about her hair, Ivana took another ten steps forward before stopping at the corner of Ursuline and Chartres Streets. She could make out the sloped roof of the house on the far end of the block, could tell by the fresh cornflower blue color of the dormer that it had received another coat of paint since she'd last seen it three years ago.

Three years ago.

It didn't seem that long, yet, in a way, it seemed like a lifetime ago. When Ivana thought about the person she'd been when she left New Orleans on that balmy summer afternoon, she had a hard time reconciling her with the woman standing on this chipped French Quarter street right now. Save for a few additional wrinkles that had popped up in the corners of her eyes and a faded scratch courtesy of a run-in with a cactus during a hike in the mountains of Hispaniola, she looked the same.

It was the *inside* that had changed.

"Not completely. You're still too much of a coward to face him."

She sucked in a deep, cleansing breath and tried to convince herself that she wasn't a coward. But as comforting —even necessary—as it occasionally was to lie to herself, it had never done her any good in the past.

If she wasn't a coward, she wouldn't have spent the past two weeks avoiding the man she was supposed to marry. She wouldn't have spent an entire night in costume two weeks ago at the kickoff party for the Diane Holmes Foundation, trailing him around the room, wondering about his relationship with the gorgeous woman he'd had on his arm.

It isn't your concern who he has on his arm.

She'd had her chance to be that person, and had thrown it away. When it came to Jonathan Campbell, she didn't have any claim on him. Zero. He was a man from her past. A man she'd loved, but one she'd run from. And if it wasn't for the fact that a close friend needed legal advice, Ivana would have done everything in her power to continue running from Jonathan.

She should have told Angus that she couldn't help him. There were other channels he could have gone through to address his situation. But it went against everything in her nature not to help a person in need. Providing aid to those in trouble was at the heart of her very existence. It's how she'd met Angus Thomson. A fellow relief worker, they'd worked alongside each other for the past three years in Haiti. So when Angus had called, frantic over an issue with his G-1 visa, Ivana couldn't help but get involved. When she realized that they needed to talk to someone with legal expertise, Jonathan was the first person who came to mind.

A chill raced through her body, and it had nothing to do

with the brisk wind still blowing off the river. She lifted the long, simple, slightly tarnished chain she kept around her neck and fiddled with the breathtaking ring that hung from it. For the past three years she'd worn the engagement ring Jonathan had given her close to her heart, treating it like a talisman, seeking strength from it when she needed courage. Ironic that she would turn to it today, when the courage she sought had to do with facing the man who'd given her the ring in the first place.

She'd envisioned the moment when she would face Jonathan again countless times, speculating about how he would react. Would he be upset? Relieved? Would he look at her as if she were a ghost? She'd tried to put herself in his position, but when she considered what *her* reaction would be to seeing someone who'd left only a week before their wedding, she could barely stomach it.

Regret coasted through her bloodstream. Thick, suffocating regret. She knew the taste of it well. It had been a healthy part of her diet for years now.

She needed to just get this over with. She would fulfill her promise to Angus, and then she would leave. Who knows, maybe Jonathan wouldn't even be around. It was late. He may have already left the office.

Ivana closed her eyes, sent up a quick prayer, and crossed the street. A mixture of anxiety and anticipation traveled along her skin as she moved ever closer to the gorgeous structure. The sun had just started its descent, turning the western sky an array of warm oranges, reds and purples.

Her heart thudded within her chest when she noticed a sleek black sedan parked in the reserved parking spot next to the law office.

Well, so much for him not being here.

She'd spent the afternoon coming up with things to do in order to delay her trip, hoping by the time she arrived everyone would be gone for the day. Jonathan had always put in way too many hours at the office. She'd gotten him out of the habit, but apparently he'd reverted back to being a workaholic.

As she approached the house, Ivana couldn't help but remember the first time she encountered Jonathan here, the very first day they met. She'd charged up the steps of the three-story creole cottage, prepared to do everything within her power to save the house from the ruin she just knew its new owner was preparing to heap upon it.

It had been determined that the house was the place where the first known voodoo healing in New Orleans had occurred, according to her sisters of the religion, which she had practiced for years. When she learned the house was slated to become a new law practice, Ivana assumed the buyer was going to gut it. Instead, he'd restored it to its former glory.

Only days after their thorny initial encounter, she'd been stunned speechless when she'd gone to dinner at the home of longtime family friend, Margo Holmes, and found herself sitting directly across the table from Jonathan Campbell. That's when Ivana learned that he was the college basketball teammate of her now brother-in-law, Tobias Holmes, her baby sister Sienna's husband.

It all seemed so, so long ago.

This little jaunt down memory lane isn't helping. Speed it up.

Ivana rolled her eyes at the annoying voice in her head, which, for some reason, did not want to get with the program when it came to stalling this inevitable meeting. But it *was* inevitable. She knew this. It was a miracle she'd managed to go the past two weeks without Jonathan discovering her presence in New Orleans. He was too tied to her family to expect this avoidance dance to go on much longer. It was time she ripped off the Band-Aid.

She climbed the porch steps and tried the door. It was locked.

Of course, it was locked. It was after normal work hours. She rang the doorbell, her heart's ridiculous racing picking up even more steam as she waited. Ivana counted a full sixty seconds before ringing it again. Maybe he wasn't here after all. It wasn't out of the realm of possibility that he left a car parked at the law firm at all times.

Just as she made the decision to leave, the door opened and the man she'd been prepared to marry appeared on the other side.

Every drop of breath she possessed seemed to rush out of her lungs. She'd seen him at the gala a few weeks ago, but always from a distance. This was the first time she'd been this close to him in three years.

The aromatic, woodsy notes of his cologne assaulted her senses, the faint smell bringing with it powerful memories of the one time in her life when she'd felt true happiness. When she'd felt loved. The weight of it was almost enough to break her.

"Hello, Jonathan," she managed to say, the words struggling past the knot of emotion wedged in her throat.

He stared at her for what seemed like an eternity. A silent, unbearably uncomfortable eternity. Those arresting, gorgeous eyes she'd spent hours gazing into as she lay languidly in his arms now looked at her with a mix of shock and aversion.

"I hope I'm not—" But before she could finish, the

alluring lilt of a woman's soft voice came from somewhere nearby.

"Jonathan, what time is the band supposed to start?" The woman arrived at the door, sidling up alongside him. "Oh, hello," she said to Ivana, her eyes wide with surprise.

Ivana took in the stunning, honey-toned beauty with legs that went on for days. She looked from the woman standing next to him in a gorgeous body-hugging gown that shimmered with thousands of crystals, to Jonathan, whom she just now realized wore a sleek, black tuxedo.

He was going out. *They* were going out. On a date.

A retched sensation settled like a lead anchor in the pit of her stomach. It wasn't as if she was surprised he was seeing someone; she'd had to put a stop to Sienna's reports on his extremely robust dating life over the years. But hearing about it from her sister while she worked in a village thousands of miles away was different from witnessing it firsthand.

"I..." Ivana started. "I didn't mean to disturb you. I just...I needed to speak with you."

The discomfort in the air was palpable as he continued to stare at her with that stoic expression. After another few moments passed, he finally said, "We're late for an event."

The iciness in his tone caused a shock of goosebumps to pop up along her skin. They were the first words he'd spoken to her in three years. To have him address her so coldly, without an ounce of feeling, was something she probably should have anticipated, but foolishly had not.

She would be lying if she said it didn't hurt. She would also be lying if she didn't admit that it was nothing less than what she deserved.

"I—" Ivana said again, but she wasn't sure how to respond. "I'm sorry for bothering you," she finally managed.

The words felt like sandpaper as they came out of her throat.

"Come by tomorrow during normal business hours," Jonathan said. He turned to the woman next to him. "Are you ready?"

"I just need to grab my clutch." She looked to Ivana. "Excuse me," she said, her eyes kind, her smile even kinder. "I love your skirt, by the way."

Ivana looked down at her bright, flowing skirt. She had a closet full of them. "Thank you," she returned.

She looked back up to find Jonathan staring at her with an emotionless expression. She'd run dozens of scenarios in her head, anticipating how he would react when they finally saw each other again. She'd readied herself for his shock. Even for his fury. But never for such...indifference. His apathy at what she considered to be one of the most significant moments she'd faced in years made her feel hollow inside.

"I should have called before coming," Ivana said once she and Jonathan were alone again.

His brows arched and he shook his head, huffing out a humorless grunt of laughter. "A call? Yeah, maybe you should have called after three years," he finished with unmistakable disdain in his voice.

Ah, there it was. There was the anger she'd anticipated.

The knot in her belly tightened by several degrees.

She'd expected this, hadn't she? Anger was an acceptable reaction when the woman who'd left you at the altar showed up on your doorstep without warning. His anger was totally justified. Still, that didn't mean it didn't hurt.

"Jonathan, I know—" Ivana started, but stopped when his date returned, carrying a sparkling royal blue clutch in her hand.

"I'm ready," the woman said. She captured Jonathan's arm and wrapped her hand around it. It wasn't an overly possessive move, yet Ivana still had a visceral reaction to seeing the woman's delicate fingers caressing his skin. Her head knew that she'd given up all rights to him the moment she'd boarded that plane to Haiti, but her heart didn't care. Her throat ached and her insides clenched with proprietorial jealousy.

Jonathan and his date stepped out onto the porch. Ivana wasn't sure why she remained standing there as he locked the door behind him. She should have left two minutes ago, after he'd so coldly told her to come back tomorrow.

Yet she remained standing there, watching as the impeccably dressed couple turned toward the stairs.

"Goodnight," the woman on his arm said. Jonathan tipped his head in a bid of farewell before escorting his date down the stairs and to the black sedan.

Ivana walked down the porch and onto the sidewalk. She stood there watching as his car backed out of the parking spot and pulled onto the street.

Her eyes connected briefly with Jonathan's as he stared at her in the rearview mirror seconds before turning onto St. Phillip Street.

"NEW ORLEANS NEEDS someone with your business savvy on the city council now that Council Member Arnold is likely moving into the mayor's office. You should think about running."

Jonathan merely smiled at the ridiculous suggestion.

As the man, whose face was familiar but whose name he didn't even try to place, continued talking, Jonathan kept up his smile, but he didn't commit to anything. He would never understand why people believed that just because a person was a good businessman it automatically meant they'd make a good politician. Some thought even bad businessmen were worthy of holding office.

Based on everything he'd experienced, it was the people who had a good sense of community that made the best public servants. Jonathan had no interest in running for office. He also had no interest in listening anymore to a virtual stranger expound on why he should.

The problem was that he was surrounded by virtual strangers.

Other than the members of the Holmes family who were in attendance tonight, this latest fundraising event for Mackenna Arnold's bid to become the next mayor of New Orleans brimmed with businesspeople and fellow politicians, all hoping to score some face time with the city's likely next mayor.

Likely? If the polls of the last few months were correct, there was no way anyone else would win this race. Mack had a double digit lead over her nearest opponent.

Jonathan had been looking forward to tonight's event. He was, after all, a businessman. And while his main purpose for being here was to support Mack's campaign, it behooved him to keep his thumb on the pulse of the city's movers and shakers. As both a lawyer and nightclub owner, it was necessary to maintain relationships with many of the people in this room. But he didn't consider any of them friends. He barely thought of them as acquaintances. They were necessary business associates. And after the episode that had taken place just a couple of hours ago on the front porch of his law practice, Jonathan wasn't in the mood to deal with any of them.

His heart still thumped with a staccato rhythm just at the thought of Ivana standing before him.

When? How? Why?

What was she doing back in the city? When had she arrived? And what in the hell did she want from him?

If Camille had not been at his side tonight, he would have left this party an hour ago. Hell, he probably wouldn't have come at all. Earlier, he hadn't made it to the next block before nearly falling victim to the compulsion to turn his car around and go back to the law office to see if Ivana was still standing on the sidewalk.

Why was she here?

Jonathan slipped his phone from his pocket and tried calling Toby again. He'd expected his best friend to be here tonight, seeing as Mackenna was soon to marry into the Holmes family. But neither Toby nor Sienna were here to support his cousin Ezra's future wife.

Jonathan had managed to corner Alex, Toby's older brother, not long after he and his wife Renee arrived, but Alex said he hadn't heard from Toby all day. He'd assumed he would see him tonight.

Of all the nights for his best friend to be missing in action...

Jonathan considered asking Alex if he knew anything about Ivana being back in New Orleans, but decided against it. The entire Holmes family knew far too much about his past with her. He didn't want anyone thinking her return affected him in any way.

But it did. Son of a bitch, did it affect him.

"Hey, there you are!" his date said, returning from the ladies' room. She carried two fresh glasses of champagne. "I took the liberty of grabbing a couple of drinks. I figured you needed one."

"Thanks," Jonathan said, accepting the flute from her. She peered around his head, looking on either side. "What are you doing?" he asked.

"Just checking to see if John Guidry talked your ears off."

Jonathan's head flew back, his deep laugh rumbling within his chest.

Camille Wright was everything he should be looking for in a companion. An attorney herself, she also owned a string of smoothie franchises throughout the southern region of Louisiana and Mississippi. Jonathan had no doubt that she had the savviest business mind in the room. She was also funny, wicked smart, and with those mile-long legs and a face like an angel, had turned more than a few heads when they'd entered tonight's function. She deserved his undivided attention tonight.

The fact that she'd agreed to accompany him to this party was a testament to just how amazing and generous she was as a person. He'd dated Camille off and on for the past year, but they weren't as close as Jonathan knew she wanted to get. Whenever it felt as if their relationship was nearing next step territory, he pulled back, usually giving her a bull-shit excuse about not being ready for anything serious. Why she still answered his calls was a mystery to him.

But she had, as much as he didn't deserve it. He owed Camille a good time tonight.

He would put that *other* woman out of his head. She'd made it more than clear three years ago that she didn't want to be the person at his side. Why in the hell should he spend his time tonight thinking about her?

Jonathan did his best to push all thoughts of Ivana to the rear of his mind.

He had a better chance of convincing himself that he

actually cared what John Guidry had to say, but he would at least put in the effort.

As he danced with Camille, he wondered what could be so important that it would spur Ivana to come unannounced to his place of business after all this time. Did she think showing up after hours would give her a better chance of being alone with him? Did she anticipate that he wouldn't want to speak to her if he had clients around? Had she wanted to avoid a scene?

Damn, there were so many different questions and scenarios swirling through his mind. He needed answers. And he didn't want to wait until she darkened his doorstep again to get them.

"What's eating at you?"

Jonathan's head shot up. He caught the concern in Camille's eyes and felt even worse for the way he'd ignored her most of the night.

"Is it the woman who came to see you right before we left?" she asked.

Yep, wicked smart.

"Don't worry about it," Jonathan said.

"Maybe you should think about taking your own advice?"

The corner of his mouth curled up in a brief smile. "I guess I deserve that."

Camille dipped her head. "Do you want to share?"

He owed her an explanation, but Jonathan knew he couldn't do it. Not right now. He shook his head. Camille responded with an understanding nod.

"If you want to cut out early, I'm okay with that," she said.

"What? No," Jonathan protested.

Yet, even as the words left his mouth, the idea of seeking out more information on Ivana quickened his blood.

"You're not as good at pretending as you think you are," Camille said. "You're barely paying attention to anyone here, Jonathan." She tipped her head back toward the double doors of the Orpheum Theater. "Go on. If anyone asks, I'll make excuses for you."

"Are you sure?" he asked. She looked at him with a raised brow. Jonathan placed a kiss on her forehead. "Thank you."

Before he could talk himself out of it, he took off for the exit, damn near sprinting to the valet. Ten minutes later he was nestled in his Tesla's bucket seats, reminding himself that getting pulled over for speeding would only slow him down. He turned onto Claiborne Avenue, heading Uptown for Toby and Sienna's house.

When he pulled up to the curb, he released a sigh of relief after spotting Toby's car in the driveway. The soft glow of a light in the front of the house shone through the sheer curtains. Jonathan hopped out of his car and hurried up the driveway to the two-story home Toby and Sienna had moved into to accompany their still growing family.

He knocked on the door, not bothering to call, seeing as Toby hadn't answered any of his previous text messages. A few seconds later, the door opened.

"Hey," Toby said, holding his new baby against his chest. "What are you doing here? I figured you'd be at Mack's fundraiser."

"I just left there," Jonathan said.

Toby glanced at the Apple Watch on his arm. "Kinda early night for you, huh?"

"Why didn't you tell me Ivana was in town?"

His best friend wasn't known for his ability to keep a straight face. It betrayed him yet again.

"Look man, I just found out last week."

"*Last week?* She's been here an entire week and you didn't think to tell me?"

The baby in Toby's arms started to wail. "Shh..." Toby cooed, gently bouncing on the balls of his feet to soothe the baby. He hitched his chin forward, indicating that Jonathan should step aside.

"Can't we go inside?" Jonathan asked.

Toby looked over his shoulder. "I've got a colicky baby, and two kids and a wife with a stomach bug in there. You don't want nothing to do with that." Toby pulled the light-weight blanket over the baby's head and joined Jonathan outside. "Look, Sienna told me last week that Ivana came home, but that's all she would say. And she specifically told me not to tell anyone."

"By anyone I assume you mean me," Jonathan said.

"I didn't ask for a list and Sienna didn't offer one. She told me not to tell *anyone* so I've kept my mouth shut."

"But why is she here after three years?"

Toby hunched his shoulders. "Sienna didn't say. The only thing she would tell me is that Ivana was coming back to New Orleans. I don't know why, or how long she'll be here." The baby started crying again.

"Bring the baby back inside," Jonathan told him. It wasn't as if he'd get anything else from Toby.

His friend nodded and turned to go back into the house, but then he spun around. "Wait. How did *you* find out Ivana was back?"

"She came to see me."

His eyes bucked. "Ivana actually went to you? When?"

"This evening, just before I left for Mackenna's

fundraiser. She didn't give me any kind of head's up or anything. She was just there, at my door, after three damn years of silence."

"Damn, man. That must have been a shock."

Understatement of the millennium.

"Well, what did she say?" Toby asked.

"She said 'hello.'"

His friend blinked. "That's it?"

"She also said that she needed to talk to me. But I'm not sure I care what she has to say," Jonathan lied.

The look Toby sent his way called him on that lie.

"Go inside," Jonathan told him again. "I'll catch up with you later. I hope Sienna and the kids are okay."

"The way things are going, I'll get sick as soon as they get over whatever it is that's turned this place into Sick People Central." Toby hitched his chin toward him. "Talk to you later."

Returning to his Tesla, Jonathan slid in and started it, but he didn't move. As he sat behind the wheel of the idling car, he wondered whether or not Ivana would actually show up tomorrow. And, if she did, what he would say to her when he saw her again.

Chapter Two

"THIS IS a bright young man you have working with you, Campbell."

"Yes, he is," Jonathan said, straightening in his chair. "Nick will make a helluva lawyer one day."

He turned to Nicolas Flores, who was so much more than just bright. The third year law student he'd been mentoring these past couple of months was one of the smartest kids Jonathan had ever met.

Jonathan made a production of hiding behind his hand as he loudly whispered toward Nicolas, "It says something when you're able to impress this old bastard."

The group of sharply dressed men at the rear table in the Port of Call restaurant all laughed. Jonathan joined in, although, if he were being honest, he'd have to admit that he hadn't paid attention to hardly anything that had been discussed over the past half hour. He hoped Nicolas had taken good notes from today's lunch meeting with the four top executives from Walker and Morris Realty.

Jonathan had worked with the group back when he lived in Charleston, more than a decade ago. The real estate investment firm had plans to expand to the Southeastern Louisiana region, and Campbell & Holmes was at the top of their list when it came to local legal representation. But they had not gotten the job yet. He'd hoped today's meeting would secure it.

Yet, instead of paying attention to the very important conversation that had taken place during their lunch, Jonathan couldn't keep his eyes from straying to the smart watch on his wrist every five seconds. The usual number of notifications lit up the tiny screen, except for the one he'd been anticipating the most.

He'd asked their receptionist, LaKeisha Lawrence, to text him when Ivana showed up at the office. It wasn't until he'd arrived this morning—a half hour earlier than usual, and with his heart racing—that he realized he hadn't given her a time to return when he'd asked her to come by today. There was something in her demeanor yesterday that suggested that whatever she wanted to discuss with him was important. He'd figured she would be there bright and early, but it looked as if she wasn't planning to show up at all.

Not that it surprised him. If there was one thing Jonathan had come to expect of Ivana, it's that she couldn't be counted on to do what she said she would do. At least that seemed to be the case whenever it came to dealing with *him*.

"Jonathan, do you take issue with having a satellite office in Baton Rouge?"

Blinking several times, he shook his head and asked, "I'm sorry, what?"

"You were scowling," Solomon Morris explained. "I wondered if it had something to do with my proposal to have a presence in Baton Rouge."

"No, no. Of course not. Setting up an office in the state's capital city is key," Jonathan said.

Shit.

If he messed this up because he'd allowed Ivana to once again mess with his head, he would give every single person in the office permission to kick his ass. Hell, he'd kick his own ass. It pissed him off that he even allowed her to still upset him at all. He shouldn't feel anything where she was concerned, anger included.

He gave his head a slight shake, and returned his focus to the matter at hand. Securing the business that Walker and Morris Realty would bring to the small law practice he shared with Harrison Holmes was what mattered right now.

Although, as Jonathan listened to his mentee, it quickly became apparent that he had nothing to worry about. He was once again blown away by the young man's poise. Most law students would be intimidated as hell speaking to a table full of multimillionaires, men who had orchestrated some of the most lucrative real estate deals of the decade. Instead, Nick gave a clinic on the inner workings of Walker and Morris. He probably knew more about the company than their executives.

Once lunch was over, Jonathan suggested they meet in another week, after he had time to draw up an official agreement. He didn't give Solomon Morris or Ronald Walker an opportunity to point out that they had not agreed to hire Campbell and Holmes as their attorneys. As far as Jonathan was concerned, they had this one in the bag.

He paid the bill and followed the older gentlemen out of the famed restaurant, walking them to a car waiting at the Esplanade Avenue entrance. The moment the black Lincoln Town Car departed the restaurant, Jonathan turned to Nicolas and clamped a hand on his shoulder.

"You were amazing."

"You think so?" Nicolas asked, the first sign of the nerves he must have been feeling showing in his eyes.

"Hell yes. You owned that lunch."

He'd started mentoring law students a while ago as a favor to a colleague who'd given up her practice in order to teach at Southern University Law Center. His first mentee had been an arrogant little shit who thought he knew everything about the law at twenty-three years old. After that first experience, Jonathan had decided mentoring wasn't for him. But when Lila contacted him a few months ago, asking if he'd be willing to give it another try with a student she thought would fit well with Jonathan's style, he'd reluctantly agreed. It was one of the best damn decisions he'd ever made. Nicolas's smarts was only surpassed by his eagerness to learn more, all while remaining humble and genuine.

They walked over to where he'd parked on Dauphine Street and got in the car, but instead of heading into the French Quarter, Jonathan turned up Barracks Street and made the block so he could drive down Esplanade Avenue and take a peek at The Hard Court, the upscale sports bar and nightclub he'd opened five years ago. He wanted to make sure the repair work being done today would be complete by the time the club opened for dinner at five. According to his security guard, a group of tourists riding Segways had motored past the building yesterday, and one had kicked up a stray rock directly into the center of the club's glass doors, shattering it.

He'd had the insurance company out first thing this morning, and had paid nearly double what the insurance covered in order to get the glass pane replaced as soon as possible. The guard had suggested sticking a piece of plywood over it, but Jonathan would be damned if he did that.

When it came to The Hard Court, he spared no expense. His club was even more lucrative than his law practice. In fact, it was so lucrative he'd decided to open another venue across town. He was scheduled to have a sit-down with his contractor later this week to go over all the specifics of what it would cost to renovate the building he'd just bought on Julia Street, in the city's Arts District.

He slowed his car as they neared the club on the other side of Esplanade and heaved out a sigh of relief at the sight of the repaired door.

"So, how do you think things went with the meeting? What's your overall impression?" Jonathan asked Nicolas as they turned onto Royal Street, heading back to the law office.

"It was pretty intimidating at first," Nicolas answered.

"You didn't let on that you were intimidated. A good poker face is essential to being a good lawyer."

"Once we dove into the details, the intimidation factor wore off. I knew I could handle that part."

"You must have studied the prospectus I gave you from cover to cover."

"All week long," Nicolas answered with a nod. "I wanted to make sure I didn't come across as being unprepared. People tend to make that assumption."

Jonathan nodded his understanding. "Sorry to be the bearer of bad news, but that never ends," he said.

It was a good thing Nicolas was aware of it. As a young Hispanic male, he would come up against people questioning his ability to do his job for the rest of his career.

Jonathan could still feel the sting of being hit with that

harsh reality years ago. Before earning his law degree, he'd spent several years playing point guard in the NBA. As a tall, athletic black man, no one questioned his ability on the court. He'd fit nicely into society's expectations in that role. But once he graduated from school and starting practicing law, everything changed. No one took him seriously. Thoughts of those early days, of how hard he had to fight for respect, still pissed him off.

"You'll be prepared for it," Jonathan said to Nicolas. "No one will be able to doubt your ability because you're showing it when you do the work. But you're not arrogant about it either," he pointed out. "You let your work speak for itself."

As he pulled into his reserved parking spot at the law practice, a discomforting throb began to beat against the walls of Jonathan's chest. He experienced that troublesome feeling whenever he thought about Ivana's out-of-the-blue appearance yesterday—something he'd thought about more in the last nineteen hours than he was willing to admit out loud.

The anticipation of seeing her again today had him in knots. He still wasn't sure *how* he should feel.

No, that wasn't true. He knew *exactly* how he should feel. He should be pissed. He should *always* be pissed when it came to Ivana Culpepper. It didn't matter how he'd once felt about her; after the shit she'd put him through, he doubted he would ever not be angry with her.

As much as it had upset him when she'd skipped town the week before their wedding, Jonathan would have been willing to forgive her. It would have taken some time, but he'd loved her too much not to give their relationship a fighting chance.

It was the fact that she hadn't even once tried to contact him that he couldn't forgive. Not a phone call or an email—not a single fucking text message. Nothing.

The only contact she'd made in these past three years was a message relayed to him by Sienna, letting him know that she had gone to another country to do relief work and that she was sorry. She wouldn't tell him what country, or how long she planned to be gone, or what she was even sorry for. He'd been prepared to spend his life with her, and she'd left him, just like that.

He was still so angry that he would be hard pressed not to lash out when he next saw her. But he wouldn't. He would do his damnedest not to show any emotion at all.

Of course, it might not even matter. She likely wouldn't bother to show up at all.

"Come to my office before you go upstairs," Jonathan told Nicolas as they climbed the steps to the law office's porch. "I have another case I want you to study. The owner finds himself in an interesting predicament regarding some old family land, and a long lost brother he didn't know he had. It's a fascinating window into Louisiana's complicated estate law."

They entered the building and Jonathan started for his office, but stopped when LaKeisha called out to him.

"Hey, before you go in there, I—" The phone rang. She held up a finger. "One minute." She took the call, directing whoever was on the other end of the line to his partner, Harrison Holmes's voicemail. She started to speak again, but another call came in.

Jonathan fixed himself a cup of coffee while he waited, offering one to Nicolas. Once done with her call, LaKeisha came over to the coffee station that sat on a side table in the parlor that served as Campbell & Holmes's lobby.

"Busy start to the afternoon, huh?" Jonathan asked.

"It's been a madhouse," LaKeisha said. "Oh, and you have a visitor in your office, though I'd rather not say her name," she finished with a bite to her tone.

He nearly choked on the coffee he'd just sipped. "Pardon me?"

"Don't worry, she hasn't been waiting long. Only ten minutes or so. I was supposed to text but then the water delivery came and there was a discrepancy with the order, and then we got bombarded with calls." She held up a hand. "Before I forget, the court date on the Nunez case has been pushed back again. I added it to your calendar, but I know how you are about checking it." She released a deep breath, her shoulders sagging. "And, so, yeah, they're in your office."

"They?" Jonathan's head lurched back. "There's two people?"

LaKeisha nodded. "I asked them to go directly to your office because I have someone coming in to give an estimate on reupholstering the furniture in the parlor." As if on cue, there was a knock at the front door. "And there he is," LaKeisha said, moving past Jonathan. "Again, sorry about not texting," she called over her shoulder.

Jonathan nodded while trying to convince his stomach to unknot. The thought of Ivana sitting in his office at this very moment sent his nerves into a tailspin.

He sucked in a fortifying breath and braced himself as he continued toward his office. This was ridiculous. He shouldn't feel nervous about seeing her again. He shouldn't feel *anything*, dammit.

He looked back at Nicolas and motioned for him to follow. "Come with me. I'll get you the files on that case I mentioned."

Jonathan entered the office and stopped short.

Ivana sat in one of the wingback chairs in the small seating area next to the window. In the opposite chair sat a guy who couldn't be older than thirty, with a mop of curly red hair that brushed against his forehead. They both held ceramic mugs and were deep in conversation, their heads tilted toward each other. It was obvious neither heard him come in.

Jonathan cleared his throat and Ivana and her companion jumped to attention. They immediately stood.

"Hello," Ivana said.

He nodded, then motioned for them to have a seat in the chairs that faced his desk. "I'll be with you in a minute."

He took more time than necessary shuffling through the files stacked neatly atop his leather blotter. He needed the extra seconds to collect himself. Once he was sure he could sit in the same room with Ivana without losing his mind, he handed several folders to Nicolas, instructing him to read over the case and be ready for a discussion later this afternoon. He waited for him to exit the office before finally turning his full attention to Ivana and her redheaded companion.

A kaleidoscope of varied sensations washed over him. The only time he ever experienced these feelings was when he was in her presence—this overwhelming sense of excitement, anticipation and awe. But now, those feelings were accompanied by a few others, the most prominent being a hostility he had a hard time containing. He cursed all these feelings to hell and fixed his features to show nothing but indifference.

Jonathan cut right to the chase. He didn't want this meeting to last a minute longer than necessary.

"You said you needed to speak to me when you came by on yesterday," Jonathan opened, settling his backside on the edge of his desk and crossing his arms over his chest. "What about?"

She sat up straighter and placed her folded hands in her lap.

"I need your help," she stated. "Well, actually, it's Angus who needs your help." She motioned to the young redhead. "I know it's somewhat bold of me to ask you for help, but I didn't know who else to turn to."

He stretched a hand out to Angus. "Jonathan Campbell."

"Angus Thomson," the man answered, his grip strong. He spoke in an accent Jonathan couldn't quite place. He'd expected to hear a Scottish brogue or a craggy Irish lilt, but this was something different. "Pleasure to meet you."

"Are you two coworkers? Friends?"

"I'm Ivana's husband."

Jonathan nearly slipped off the desk, his limbs suddenly going weak. Shock ricocheted throughout his body.

"*Not* my husband," Ivana quickly interjected. "We don't have to say that anymore, remember?"

"Oh, yes. Yes, sorry. I forgot." Angus shook his head, his pale skin taking on a pinkish hue. "We're not really married."

Jonathan swallowed past the knot of painful, indescribable emotion wedged in his throat. "Either of you care to explain exactly what's going on here?" he asked.

"This may take a while to explain," Ivana said. "Are you sure you want to get into the details right now? I know this is last minute. It's okay if you need us to come back when you have more time in your schedule."

"You're here," Jonathan said. "I'd like to avoid you coming back at all if possible."

She flinched.

Jonathan's first instinct was to apologize for his curt tone, but he fought the urge. His delivery could have been less harsh, but he meant the words. He agreed to see her this one time, but he didn't want Ivana coming around.

She nodded. "That's fair." She sucked in a deep breath, then slowly released it. "Let me start by reassuring you that Angus and I are not married. I'd suggested it as a possible solution to his staying in the country, but we both know it isn't right. That's why we're here now. We're hoping you can provide some legal advice. That's all I'm asking for. Advice and nothing else."

THE POUNDING in her chest was reminiscent of how her heart would race after a five mile trek through the mountains of Hispaniola. As she listened to Angus explaining his dilemma, Ivana fought to control the nerves roiling in the pit of her stomach. She'd debated the wisdom of coming here. She had prepared Angus beforehand, cautioning him that they were likely to receive a no from Jonathan.

But that hadn't happened. Yet.

In all honesty, she was surprised they were even still here. Ivana had fully expected Jonathan to dismiss them based on the simple fact that this wasn't his area of legal expertise. Instead, he'd sat in the leather-covered desk chair and asked for more information. And Angus, being Angus, took it as an invitation to tell an abbreviated version of his life story.

Granted, it was a remarkable life story. At first glance, one would never expect the baby-faced redhead, with peaches and cream skin and adorable freckles, to have spent his adolescence living with his missionary parents in Thailand and Indonesia after spending his formative years in his birthplace of Johannesburg.

Angus's plurinational background was the reason they were here today. His South African and Thai passports had both been flagged at some time during his years of relief work in Haiti, which had caused some sort of hiccup with his US visa status. He had exactly one week before he would be forced to leave the country. The problem was that the woman of his dreams, a beautiful Thai girl he'd gone to high school with, was currently in Los Angeles, studying medicine at UCLA. It was Angus's hope to spend his two-month sabbatical from relief work visiting Phawta and to propose to her on her birthday in April. This business with his G-1 diplomatic visa status put a huge wrinkle in his plans.

"I thought if Ivana and I were married, it would at least give me more time in the country," Angus was saying now. "People do it all the time, you know."

"But I pointed out to him that it wasn't realistic, nor is it legal," Ivana said.

"I don't think Phawta would like it either," Angus said.

"No, she would not," she agreed. She looked to Jonathan. His expressionless eyes seemed to look right through her, as if she were a stranger. Clearing the emotion in her throat that had welled up out of nowhere, Ivana said, "I know this isn't your area of expertise, but I was hoping you could give us some direction on how to go about straightening things out with his visa."

"Before we go any further, maybe I should explain to him what happened the last time I tried to get a dual intent visa," Angus interjected.

"That sounds like an important part of the story," Jonathan said, motioning for him to continue.

While Angus resumed his account of his immigration woes, Ivana's eyes roamed the office, soaking in the familiarity of it. How many times had she visited him here in the two years they were together? Too many to count.

And because torturing herself with the memories she'd made with Jonathan had become her new pastime since her return to New Orleans, it was inevitable that her mind would drift to some of the things they'd done together in this office. Those stolen moments they'd shared when she would slip away from the stand where she sold incense in the French Market, just a couple of blocks away. They'd blessed every surface of this office, making love on top of the desk, in his desk chair, on the sofa that once sat against the wall near the fireplace.

Ivana looked over to the area where the sofa once stood and realized it had been replaced by a sideboard table. Then she looked closer at his desk and noticed that it too had been replaced. The previous one had been made of a much darker wood, a rich mahogany that she'd helped him pick out during a shopping trip at the antique shops in St. Francisville. That desk had cost over three thousand dollars, and was the type that should have lasted him for decades, not just a few years.

A noxious feeling began to develop in her stomach when she realized the chair he now sat in was different too. Had he purposely expunged everything in this office that reminded him of her? Was it his intent to erase all the memories they'd made?

Maybe she was reading too much into this. There was probably a perfectly good explanation behind his decision to change out all the furniture. Maybe there had been a water leak that ruined the previous desk, chair and sofa. It had happened once before and he'd been forced to repair a portion of the ceiling and the hardwood floors.

She looked up at the ceiling, searching for any sign that work had been done on it. It hadn't. This ceiling was the same. There was a slightly off-white swatch, a remnant of the previous repair job. Ivana was well acquainted with that spot. It resided directly in her line of vision whenever he would lay her back on his desk.

She sucked in a painful breath at the memory.

When she looked to Jonathan, she found him staring at her with a raised brow. He glanced up at the ceiling, a questioning look on his face. Ivana would rather die than to have him figure out the thoughts that had been going through her head.

"So, do you think you can help Angus?" she asked.

"First, I need to know how much you charge per hour?" Angus interjected. "Helping to rebuild homes in Haiti is rewarding, but the pay is not."

"I told you not to worry about the money," Ivana said. She turned to Jonathan. "I'm going to help him with the legal fees in whatever way I can. It's important that he is able to spend time with Phawta."

"She's right," Angus said. "We only have six weeks left before we have to return."

Jonathan's eyes widened. "You're here for another six weeks?"

The perturbed edge to his tone stung. She sat up straight, lifting her chin slightly.

"I'm not sure how long I'll be here," Ivana said, answering as truthfully as she could without giving away too much. Her time at home was still up in the air. "A relief group that normally works in Guatemala is currently serving our village, but they will be leaving soon."

"I have to go to Phawta before I go back to Haiti," Angus pleaded. "I haven't seen my girl since we met up in Thailand to celebrate Songkran. That was ten months ago. I can't take a chance flying to California with my passport situation the way it is, and it would take me days to drive there."

"He also doesn't have a driver's license, so he *can't* drive there," Ivana said in an admonishing voice.

"That too," Angus said.

"Is there anything that can be done?" Ivana asked.

Jonathan leaned back in his chair and rapped his pen against the desk. Several long moments stretched between them before he tossed the pen aside, straightened in his chair and folded his hands over the blotter on his desk.

"As you know, this isn't the kind of law I practice. However," he said, his attention on Angus, "karma may be seeking a way to reward you for the good deeds you've performed as a relief worker. I happen to have a friend who practices immigration law. In fact, she was just at the border last week, aiding families seeking asylum."

He pressed a button on the desk phone and the monotone hum of the open phone line filled the air. He dialed a number and after three rings, a man picked up.

"Serena Dayton's office."

"Hi Chad, this is Jonathan Campbell. Is Serena available?"

"Hello, Mr. Campbell. She's finishing up a conference call. I'll let her know you're on hold."

They waited a couple of seconds before someone picked up on the other end of the line.

"Well, hello stranger." The sultry voice that emerged

from the phone's speaker cause uncomfortable pinpricks to dance along Ivana's skin. "I wondered what a woman had to do to hear back from you. To what do I owe the pleasure of this call? Or is it you who's seeking pleasure this time?"

Jonathan had the presence of mind to look uncomfortable. He cleared his throat.

"It's...umm...not that kind of call," he said. "I'm seeking your *professional* advice this time. I have two people in my office—who can hear this conversation since I have you on speakerphone, by the way—and one is having an issue with a visiting visa."

"Why didn't you say that, Jonathan." The woman's tone instantly became more businesslike, but the sensual familiarity in her initial greeting would haunt Ivana for a long time to come. It didn't take a rocket scientist to figure out that he and the woman on the other end of the line were far more than just professional acquaintances.

As Jonathan explained Angus's situation to the other lawyer, Ivana stared at the floor, unable to meet his eyes. If she looked at him, he would know that she was torturing herself by imagining him with this other woman.

Had he been with her in this office? Did Serena Dayton have memories of staring at the discolored patch on the ceiling while Jonathan sent her to heaven and back?

Ivana pressed a hand to her stomach, which suddenly felt as if it was going to reject the grilled shrimp salad she'd eaten for lunch. She'd known coming here would be a special kind of agony, but it was so much worse than she'd first imagined.

"We're working within a very short timeframe," Jonathan explained. "Angus here has less than a week. Do you think you can work your magic?"

"I'll see what I can do," Serena said.

"I knew I could count on you," Jonathan said.

"Maybe you can buy me a drink at The Hard Court next week as a thank you," the woman replied, a tint of that earlier sultriness returning to her voice.

Ivana glanced up to see a slight, knowing grin curl up the side of Jonathan's mouth. "It would be my pleasure," he answered.

If given the chance, Ivana would levitate from this chair and fly right out the window. Having to sit here and endure his sensual banter with a woman he'd obviously been intimate with was more than her already bruised heart could withstand.

As hard as it had been to ignore his relationships while she lived over a thousand miles away, it would be impossible to escape them now that she was back in this city. Her only option was to refrain from being in the same space with him. Of course, that feat would be just as impossible to accomplish, seeing as he was her brother-in-law's best friend.

The lump of regret and discomfort clogging her throat made it hard to swallow. But whose fault was that? It wasn't Jonathan's. He had every right to flirt with whomever he chose, gallivanting from one woman to another. She'd handed that right to him the moment she chose to run away.

Ivana could laugh when she thought about the little fantasy that had been running through her head since the fall, from the moment she realized she would finally return to her hometown after three long years. She'd never been brave enough to say it out loud, but she'd indulged in it countless times in the months leading up to her flight to New Orleans.

The fantasy that she and Jonathan would find their way

back to each other. How foolish had she been to have ever considered it a possibility.

She'd made this lonely bed for herself when she ran away from him. It was only fair that she must now lie in it. Alone.

Chapter Three

SHE SHOULD PROBABLY SWITCH to the other side.

The thought had occurred to her more than once. If she stayed like this much longer she'd have the throw pillow's thick cord imprinted on her face.

"So what," Ivana muttered as she stared at the television. She'd been in the same position for the past hour, lounging on her mother's "good" sofa with her cheek smushed up against the pillow's scratchy embroidery. If Sylvia Culpepper were to walk through that door right now, she'd have the hissy fit to end all hissy fits.

But her mother was out of town for the weekend, off to some convention with women from her college sorority. Ivana had full reign over this stuffy house without the threat of getting into an argument. Yet, she still couldn't get comfortable. She was never comfortable in her mother's home, even as a child.

She really, *really* needed to get out of here. She'd thought—hoped—that after three years, maybe she and Sylvia could find some semblance of peace and civility when it came to their relationship. She should have known that after sixty-eight years, her mother wouldn't change. Ivana had spent the past two weeks holding her tongue while her mother offered dozens of unsolicited opinions about the state of her middle daughter's life.

Thank goodness the renter currently occupying her Granny Elise's house in Bywater would be moving out next week. Her grandmother had left the house to Sienna, but Ivana knew her sister wouldn't have a problem with her staying there. Sienna had always felt guilty about inheriting the house while Ivana and their older sister, Tosha, had been left with nothing but a few savings bonds.

Ivana had promised to stay there only until Sienna found a new tenant. But...maybe not.

She stifled another sigh.

The status of her stay in New Orleans was still up in the air. So far, she'd stuck to the narrative she'd devised before leaving Haiti; that she would return to the island nation in another six weeks with the rest of the members of her team. However, during their last conversation before Ivana left the village, her supervisor at Operation: Heal had suggested she take a much longer break, no less than a year. If she chose to come back at all.

Ivana's breath hitched even now.

She knew better than to brush aside the woman's words. Patience Edwards was both a colleague and a friend, and after working with the organization for more than thirty years, she understood the strain of relief work better than most. It took a toll on one's body.

Patience constantly encouraged the relief workers under her tutelage to give themselves wellness breaks, but the thought of taking weeks for herself had seemed selfish to Ivana. The people they were helping didn't have the luxury of taking a break away from their lives. Why should she?

She'd learned the answer to that question several months ago, when she awoke in the middle of the night to what she'd thought was a heart attack. It had turned out to be a stress-induced anxiety attack, but it had put the fear of God in her.

Pushing aside her own stubbornness—something Ivana could admit had not been easy—she'd finally given in to her supervisor's demands and treated herself to a week on the touristy side of the island, at an all-inclusive resort in the Dominican Republic. It had been glorious, but the guilt over spending those few days in such luxury had eaten Ivana up inside. Only a month later, she found herself suffering yet another panic attack. It was then that she realized she was putting her own health at risk. She'd agreed to join Angus, Bethany and Roger Smith, and the tattooed Englishman they all called Goose, on a two-month wellness break.

Ivana wasn't sure the stress of being back home wasn't as bad as what she'd endured in Haiti. If she didn't move into Granny Elise's house soon, she would likely suffer her third panic attack.

A notification popped up on her phone, reminding her that the winter coat giveaway she'd volunteered to help with at the New Orleans Mission would be starting in another half hour. She stared at the message for several moments before swiping her finger across the screen and deleting it. She set the phone down on Sylvia's spotless glass coffee table, and refused to allow guilt to overwhelm her yet again. She knew some of the other people volunteering for this afternoon's giveaway. The event was in capable hands.

Burnout.

That's what she was in the midst of. She'd spent the

past fifteen years giving everything she had to others. Right now, she just didn't have anything left to give.

This attitude felt so different from her usual mode of operation, but she *was* different. There was no denying it. She just didn't have it in her to stand there for hours, handing out overcoats and smiling a smile she didn't feel. She'd rather put lumps in her mother's precious throw pillow while she binged-watched the reboot of *One Day at a Time* on Netflix.

Of course, if she were out with other people, experiencing their joy at receiving something they desperately needed, she wouldn't have time to think back on the hour she'd spent in Jonathan's office yesterday. She wouldn't have the sultry voice of his lawyer friend resonating in her head. She wouldn't be lying here constantly imagining just how close the two of them had gotten over the years.

Had they started out as colleagues, or had they been in a serious relationship from the very beginning? Was it ever *really* serious, or had it been just a friends with benefits thing? Did he harbor feelings for this woman to this day?

None of this was her concern, yet thoughts of Jonathan's relationship with Serena Dayton continued to plague her. Last night, she'd succumbed to the temptation to look her up online. Unsurprisingly, the woman was gorgeous. Drop dead, stunningly gorgeous.

And, of course, she had more than just looks going for her. Based on the dozens of articles from local news outlets and various legal trade publications, she was also outrageously successful and, if her Twitter feed was anything to go by, a true social justice warrior. Heck, she'd agreed to look into Angus's situation without a moment's hesitation. Ivana owed Serena Dayton a debt of gratitude.

Gratitude was *not* what she felt toward the attorney at

the moment. The same could be said for the woman who had been on Jonathan's arm at the masquerade ball for the Diane Holmes Foundation a few weeks ago, and the one in that exquisite blue gown who'd accompanied him to whatever function he'd attended the other night. When she thought about any of those women, the only emotion Ivana could summon was jealousy. They, after all, had the one thing she wanted the most.

He isn't yours.

The reminder was the slap in the face she needed. Jonathan Campbell had been hers at one time, but she no longer held claim to him. She could not—*would not*—hold it against any woman who jumped at the chance she'd so foolishly tossed away.

The one thing yesterday's visit to the Law Office of Campbell and Holmes had made abundantly clear was that no matter what she decided to do with her future—whether it was returning to Haiti, or changing her career direction toward something entirely different—it would be too painful to remain in New Orleans. She'd thought she could handle being near Jonathan again, but given the turmoil she'd felt since leaving his office yesterday, it was clear she'd made a faulty calculation.

That, of course, begged another question. What *was* she going to do with the rest of her life?

Goodness, could this situation be anymore pathetic? How could a woman knocking on forty still be asking herself what she wanted to do when she grew up? She had never felt so directionless. Not even a decade ago, when she quit her high-paying corporate job after suffering her very first panic attack.

Ivana sat up straight.

Why had it just occurred to her that what she'd experienced in Haiti was practically the same thing that happened to her before leaving her old job? Maybe it wasn't the relief work that had brought about her near breakdown. Maybe it was *her*. Maybe it was just her nature to flat out lose her mind when life started to overwhelm her.

"Great," she muttered. "Only took you nearly four decades to figure that out."

Her phone chimed again, but this time with a text from Sienna.

Get dressed. We're going out. Pick you up in an hour.

Ivana groaned. She'd hoped now that her sister was married with children, she wouldn't have to worry about Sienna pestering her about her lack of a social life. Another message came through.

Wear something hot. You're getting lucky tonight.

It was followed by three emojis: a dancing lady in a red dress, a glass of wine and an eggplant.

Ivana rolled her eyes. There would be no eggplant in her immediate future, not unless they were going to an Italian restaurant that served it breaded and covered in red sauce and parmesan cheese.

She shut off Netflix and went into her room to search through the suitcase she still hadn't fully unpacked. It was silly not to at least put her underwear in drawers. But other than a few skirts she'd hung in the closet out of necessity— or rather, her sheer abhorrence of having to use an iron— Ivana refused to put her clothes away. As much as she appreciated being able to stay at her mother's home, she didn't want to feel as if she'd moved in. She vowed to be out of here the first chance she got.

She dropped her hands to her sides and stared up at the ceiling. She'd been having this same conversation with herself since she was fifteen years old. When it came to full-circle moments, this one sucked.

She returned her attention to the overstuffed suitcase, picking through her clothes to find a suitable outfit for whatever her sister had in mind. She wanted to be dressed by the time she arrived. Anything to avoid a confrontation with Sienna's pushy behind.

It was unseasonably warm for this time of year—even for New Orleans—so Ivana opted for a turquoise tank top with beautiful, hand sewn beads along the rim of the collar, overlaid with her gauzy, sheer peach blouse, and a flowing skirt that contained both colors and about a dozen more.

She added moisturizer to her hair in an attempt to tame it, but the volume wouldn't decrease, no matter how much lotion she slathered on. She ran to the kitchen and put her head underneath the sink's high, gooseneck faucet, then saturated her scalp with a variety of products for natural hair. Brushing it into a sleek, wavy ponytail, she captured her hair in a jeweled clip just behind her left ear, letting the ponytail rest on her shoulder.

After adding just enough makeup to make her not feel like a mummy, Ivana dabbed a hint of ylang ylang behind her ears and at her wrists, then went back to the living room to finish up the episode of *One Day at a Time* that she had been watching while she waited for Sienna. Just as she sat down, she heard the front door opening.

"Hey, are you ready?" Sienna called from the front of the house.

Wait! She had a key? How had she managed that? Sylvia had made it known a long time ago that her house was *her* house, and once her daughters moved out they were guests. Ivana had been staying here for nearly a week before she was able to pry a key from her mother.

"Oh, I like that top," Sienna said as she approached. "Both of them."

"Thanks," Ivana said. She pointed to her sister's cute black dress that she'd paired with stylish red pumps. "Why are you dressed like you're hoping to catch a man?"

"Because my man will be there tonight and I want to look good for him." She shook her hips. "And make every other man fawn over me, of course."

Ivana couldn't help but laugh. Her baby sister's confidence had shot into the stratosphere after she'd gotten married, which was a very good thing. She cherished her brother-in-law for a number of reasons, but most of all for making her sister so damn happy.

Ivana grabbed her purse before following Sienna toward the front door. "So, where are we going?"

"Out," her sister replied.

"I know that." Ivana locked the door behind them. "Where to?"

She turned to find Sienna standing at the base of the concrete steps leading up to her mother's front door, a pensive frown marring her forehead.

Ivana narrowed her eyes. "Cee Cee, where are you taking me?"

"The Hard Court," she finally answered. She put her hands up. "I know it's probably the last place you want to go, but this is a huge night for Toby. This new Kpop group he discovered on YouTube is debuting there tonight. He needs as much love and support as possible."

Ivana had no idea what a Kpop was, but her sister was right about one thing: The Hard Court was the absolute *last* place she wanted to be right now. Her emotions were still raw following yesterday's visit to Jonathan's office. She could use a couple of days before she had to see him again.

But would a couple of days make much of a difference? She was here for another six weeks at the very least—possibly much, much longer. It was unrealistic to think she could avoid Jonathan.

That doesn't mean you have to walk directly into the lion's den.

Although, when she thought about it, she realized she had a good chance of avoiding him tonight. Based on what she remembered, he tended to move around the club, going from table to table, checking in on patrons. When he wasn't on the floor, he spent much of his time in his personal suite upstairs, with its smoke gray windows that allowed him to look out over the entire main floor of the club. If her luck was worth anything at all, that's where he would be tonight.

"It's fine," Ivana said. "Let's go."

Her sister's eyes widened into huge brown orbs, which told Ivana that Sienna hadn't expected her to capitulate so easily. She hoped she didn't live to regret it.

She climbed into the massive SUV and tossed a crocheted baby rabbit into one of the three car seats lined up in the middle row. Ivana sat through two solid minutes of a song about a baby shark before reminding her sister that her kids weren't in the car, so they didn't have to listen to their music.

They hopped onto the Pontchartrain Expressway and then exited a few minutes later. As they drove through Treme, toward Jonathan's club just on the edge of the French Quarter, Ivana could still remember the visceral reaction she'd had after learning a nightclub would be coming to such a historic part of the city. As was the case so many times when it came to Jonathan in those earlier days, she'd prejudged both him and his club. The Hard Court fit right in with the neighborhood. It brought life to the area, along with a significant boost to local businesses.

Despite the mental pep talk she'd given herself before leaving the house, she became more anxious the closer they inched toward the club. Tonight would be a test of her strength. If she could get through this evening without wanting to lock herself in the ladies room and hurl, maybe she could consider moving back to New Orleans permanently.

Surviving in this city without Jonathan as her significant other would be hard. Having to see him with other women would be even harder. But if she passed tonight's test, maybe it wouldn't be so bad.

The lies we tell ourselves.

"This is new," Ivana said as they turned onto the side street. A two-story parking structure sat directly behind the club. Instead of the typical, drab concrete, the parking garage was made of sleek steel. Thick green foliage cascaded from flower boxes that peppered the facade, transforming the otherwise cold structure into a work of art.

"Jonathan had it built about a year ago," Sienna said, pulling into a spot marked *Reserved.* "Trying to find street parking turned into a nightmare with all the new shops and restaurants that have opened in this area. This has helped to alleviate some of it. The residents here sure are grateful."

"I guess he really has made a positive impact on the city," Ivana murmured.

She worked hard to manage the regret that tried to suffocate her whenever she thought about what she'd missed out on by leaving three years ago, but losing the opportunity to witness all Jonathan had done for both of his businesses and, in turn, for the city of New Orleans, was a regret she would hold for as long as she walked this earth.

A covered walkway led from the new parking garage to the front entrance. As she entered through the glass doors, Ivana was pummeled with a tidal wave of nostalgia. Unlike his law office, very little had changed here.

Of course, it was hard to improve upon perfection. Toby's cousin, interior designer Indina Holmes, had nailed Jonathan's vision of an upscale, basketball-themed sports bar. The polished wood of the main dance floor glistened like that of a spanking new basketball court. An array of seating areas occupied the perimeter, with several private booths tucked into cozy alcoves. The second floor housed the bistro, with more tables set around the open balcony that overlooked the first floor.

Ivana took a moment to collect herself. The energy of the crowd, the thumping music from the deejay, it all brought about a mélange of memories that threatened to overwhelm her. The first time Sienna dragged her to this club, it was to support one of Toby's musical acts, just as they were doing tonight. She had a feeling this rush of déjà vu would happen a lot over the course of the evening.

"They're probably over there," Sienna said, pointing toward the right side of the club. The place seemed to be at capacity already, even though it wasn't yet nine o'clock.

They moved toward the massive crowd congregating near one of the intimate nooks against the far wall. There were only four such areas in the club, each bracketed by sheer curtains that could be closed for privacy. Following Sienna as she maneuvered her way through the throng, Ivana soon discovered the source of the excitement emanating from the onlookers that had converged on the secluded seating area.

R&B superstar, Aria Jordan, sat on the edge of the U-shaped couch, posing for a selfie with a group of women wearing tiaras and satin sashes across their chests. Just five years ago, Ivana had been here at The Hard Court when Aria made her debut on a reality TV show; a still wet-behind-the-ears Toby as her manager. *A Week in the Life of a Wannabe Star* launched both Aria and Toby's careers. The girl now had several gold records to her name, and would soon headline her own concert tour.

"Ivana! Wow!" Aria jumped up from her seat. "It's been so long since I've seen you." She greeted Ivana with a bear hug, which caused a number of the people in the crowd to start taking pictures of Ivana, as if she were a star by osmosis or something. Celebrity was an amazing and extremely weird thing these days.

"I was hoping we could enjoy the show down here," Toby said from his place on the opposite side of the plush bench. "But we may have to move upstairs."

"I think we're good," Aria said. "They'll turn their attention to the stage once iKonik starts performing."

Ivana doubted Aria's adoring fans would be distracted by some unknown pop band, but what did she know? She'd thought the same years ago when Aria Jordan had been the unknown, and look at her now.

Toby ordered a round of drinks and, after about a half hour with no sign of the club's owner, Ivana finally started to relax. Toby's newest find took to the stage just past ten o'clock. The crowd went insane. Ivana still had no idea what Kpop was, but iKonik seemed to hit all the checkmarks on the boy band checklist: cute faces, flashy, choreographed dance moves, and smooth voices that harmonized to perfection. If she closed her eyes, she could have sworn she was listening to a 90's R&B group.

She'd just started to feel okay with Sienna dragging her here tonight when she glanced over and noticed Jonathan walking toward them. She instinctively shirked back against the sofa cushion, attempting to make herself as small as possible.

No. Don't you do that.

She was done being a coward. She sat up straight and relaxed her shoulders. At least she hoped she looked relaxed on the outside. Inside, her nerves twisted and turned in her stomach.

Toby stood, greeting Jonathan with a one-armed hug. They turned to the stage, where the band had begun an encore of the song they'd just finished. She hadn't been directly in Jonathan's line of sight when he'd walked over, so Ivana couldn't be sure he'd even noticed her. She, however, was acutely aware of every single twitch he made.

At least he was alone tonight. She wouldn't have to suffer the heartache of watching him with another woman.

And then, just like that, he wasn't alone.

The woman who'd accompanied him to whatever event he'd attended the other night when Ivana had gone to his office sidled up to him and put her arm around his waist. Apparently, Toby hadn't realized Jonathan had a date tonight. Ivana could tell by the way he visibly stiffened and how he moved slightly to the left to try to shield her from their view.

Goodness but she loved her brother-in-law.

She peered over at Sienna and caught the look of pure disgust on her sister's face. Ivana signaled with a short wave and shook her head. She didn't want a scene. The last thing tonight needed was her sister going off on Jonathan.

This was *his* club. He had the right to bring whomever he wanted here with him. Ivana would have to deal with this countless times in the future. It was best she get used to it.

The band brought their final song to a close and the crowd showered them with raucous applause, so boisterous it felt as if the building was shaking.

"Your acts are forever bringing the heat to my club," Jonathan said, clamping his arm around Toby's shoulder as they turned to face the seating area. His smile faltered when he caught sight of Ivana.

That urge to cower overpowered her once again, but she maintained her outward composure. On the inside, her discomfort was so acute Ivana felt it in her bones.

Jonathan tugged his date closer to his side, spanning her waist with his arm and settling his hand on her hip.

The lump in Ivana's throat magnified, little pieces of her soul dying inside as his actions delivered the message loud and clear.

"Why don't we all go upstairs?" he asked. "I'll have the kitchen whip up some hors d'oeuvres.

"I should get home to the kids," Sienna said, her words clipped. "Vonnie, are you ready?"

"I thought the kids were spending the night at Mom and Gerald's?" Toby asked.

Sienna flashed him a death glare. He flinched, then glanced at Ivana. "Oh. Umm, yeah. You're right," Toby said. "You should probably get back."

Despite the intense desire to grab hold of the opportunity Sienna had handed her, Ivana didn't want to take the coward's way out yet again. Instead, she said, "That's okay if you have to leave. I'll take an Uber when I'm ready to go home."

If she was in the mood to laugh, Ivana would have broken a rib at the shocked looks plastered on the faces around her. But laughing was the absolute last thing she was in the mood to do right now. It took every single ounce of fortitude she possessed to put up this brave front.

"Uh, okay," Sienna said, a perplexed frown pulling down the edges of her mouth. "I guess Margo can handle the kids for the rest of the night."

"Good," Ivana said. She pushed up from the sofa and forced herself to smile. "Are we going upstairs?"

Jonathan and his date led the way to his private suite, which afforded the best view in the club. As she followed, Ivana could only hope she could keep up this performance a little while longer. Lord knows it was the toughest acting job of her life.

JONATHAN STOOD in the center of the long-vacant warehouse at the corner of Julia and Constance Streets, in the heart of the city's Arts District. The interior of the three story structure was still in decent shape, a miracle seeing as it hadn't seen an occupant since Hurricane Katrina. Based on what he knew from his experience renovating his law practice, he now suspected this renovation wouldn't take nearly as much work as he first thought. Or, at least he hoped it wouldn't.

Jonathan heard someone emit a low whistle, then proclaim in a deep voice, "I know you paid a pretty penny for this place. It's gorgeous."

He turned to find Alexander Holmes striding across the concrete floor, followed closely by another man of equal height, but not as much bulk as Alex. Both wore polo shirts with *Holmes Construction* embroidered on the pocket.

Jonathan held his hand out, clasping Alex's in a firm shake and bringing him in for a one-arm hug.

"Thanks for coming out," Jonathan said.

"Thanks for hiring Holmes Construction for this job," Alex replied.

As if he'd even think about going with another contractor. The fact that Alex was practically family didn't play a part in his decision to hire him; it's because Holmes Construction was the best in the city. Hands down. And when it came to this project, Jonathan wanted the best.

"This is Travis Hawkins," Alex said, introducing the man who'd accompanied him. "He'll be the foreman on this project. The lead engineer is on her way. She's meeting with a client on the West Bank, but it should be wrapping up pretty soon."

"Sounds good," Jonathan said. "Just a warning, I may have to skip out a bit early. I have a meeting back at the office in about forty minutes, but if you have anything in particular that you need me to clear up you can always text or send a message through LaKeisha."

Alex waved him off. "This initial assessment is just to give us an idea of what we'll be working with. Based on what you want to do with this place, I doubt it'll take the entire eight months you mentioned."

"I want to *open* in eight months," Jonathan said. "Indina will need at least two months to work her magic after you're done."

"I wouldn't worry about that. Indina can take a decrepit pile of junk and make it look like a mansion within a week," Alex said. "I told her she needs to start one of those design shows on TV."

Jonathan laughed. He'd been telling Indina the same thing for years. She definitely had the personality for it.

She'd bring a fresh perspective to all those house flipping shows his sister, Jacqueline, loved to watch. That reminded him, he owed his twin a phone call. She'd been on her way to a 76ers game when he called last night, and nothing came between her and her basketball.

"What made you want to open a nightclub in this part of the city?" Alex asked as they walked toward the far end where Jonathan had envisioned a large, circular bar. "Are you sure that kind of crowd would fit in this area?"

"This won't be that kind of club," Jonathan said. "Think more laid back. Relaxed."

As he examined the space, it was hard not to think about Ivana and how she'd inspired his newest venture.

Don't think about her.

He'd expended an insane amount of effort to jettison all thoughts of Ivana Culpepper from his mind. Thinking about her would bring back memories of the hurt he'd glimpsed in her soulful eyes last night when he'd tightened his arm around Camille's waist.

Jonathan wasn't even sure why he'd done it. To hurt her? To show his friends that he didn't need her? To show *himself* that he didn't need her?

Once they'd gone up to his private suite at the club, he'd attempted a course correct, putting some distance between himself and Camille. Not that it had mattered. Ivana had mostly ignored him, spending the rest of the night chatting with Aria Jordan and then with Monica and Eli Holmes, who'd arrived in time for iKonik's encore performance.

Still, that flash of hurt he'd witnessed in her eyes remained with him. He couldn't get that vision out of his head.

Why was she here? Why couldn't she have stayed in Honduras or Haiti or wherever the hell she'd run off to when she'd left him? Having her back in New Orleans stirred up feelings he'd vowed never to feel again, toward *any* woman. He'd be damned if he fell victim to them again.

Alana Sanders, Holmes Construction's lead engineer, arrived, and Jonathan forced thoughts of Ivana out of his head. He needed to focus on business.

He started to breathe easier after a half hour of touring the warehouse. Alex and his team knocked on the walls, inspected the beams and gave the space a cursory overview, deciding that, overall, the building was solid. Jonathan wasn't naive enough to expect smooth sailing throughout this process. He'd learned during the renovations of both The Hard Court and his law practice that there were always hiccups along the way. But as long as those hiccups didn't blow his budget clean out of the water, or add months of extra time to the job before it could be completed, he was ready to take whatever this warehouse handed him. In the end, he would have a night spot unlike anything New Orleans had ever seen.

Several months ago, he'd flown overseas to visit a number of gentlemen's clubs throughout Europe after finally deciding to go ahead with the idea he'd been mulling over for the past couple of years. There were only a few in the United States that even came close to the type of establishment he planned to open. But, unlike those clubs, his would not be exclusive to men.

"Hey, do you have everything you need here?" Jonathan asked Alex. "I need to get back to the office."

"I want to stay a little while longer. We'll take some measurements and a few pictures, then my team and I can start working up a plan."

"No problem," Jonathan said, handing Alex the key. "I can drive over to your office to pick the key up later today."

"Actually, I'm meeting up with Harrison after work," Alex said. "We've been putting off getting together for weeks now, and both our wives told us that we'd better take some time to meet up or they're not letting us back in the house."

"Good for them," Jonathan said with a laugh. "Harrison's been trying hard to relax, but it's not easy to give up being a workaholic when it's been your way of life for so long. I'm happy you're there to help him. He needs it."

"We both do." Alex held up the keys. "I'll drop these off when I come by to see Alex. The estimate for time, materials and the cost of the reno should be done by next week."

Jonathan left Alex and his team at the warehouse, driving down South Peters toward his office. Just as he pulled into his parking spot, his phone rang with the law practice's number. "I'm outside," Jonathan answered. "You can show Chris Barton to my office."

"He had to cancel," LaKeisha said. "He just called."

Well, shit. He could have stayed at the warehouse a bit longer with Alex and the rest of the Holmes Construction crew.

"However, Angus Thomson is here to see you," his receptionist continued.

Jonathan stopped in the middle of opening his car door. "Did he say why?"

Although, the question he *really* wanted to ask was whether or not Angus was alone, or had he come with Ivana.

"No, but I can ask," LaKeisha said. "All he said was that he only had a short time and wanted to speak with you."

Jonathan entered the law office and walked directly to his receptionist's desk. "You mind ordering lunch for the office?" he asked.

"My pick?"

"Yeah. Just none of that Greek food," Jonathan pleaded.

"You will learn to appreciate a good gyro." She cocked her chin toward the side parlor. "Mr. Thomson is in there."

"Thanks," Jonathan said. On his way to the parlor, he spotted Nicolas coming out of the downstairs conference room.

"What are you doing here?" Jonathan asked. "I thought you had that seminar?"

"Cancelled. The entire panel of speakers got food poisoning last night," Nicolas said. He held up the file in his hand. "I've found some pretty interesting things in here. Let me know when you have time to talk about it."

"As soon as I'm done with Mr. Thomson," Jonathan said, motioning to Angus. He shook the man's hand, his entire being sagging in relief upon discovering he'd come alone. "Should we go to my office?" Jonathan asked.

"Actually, this won't take long," Angus replied. "I only have a few minutes, but I couldn't leave without thanking you personally for your help. Ms. Dayton took care of everything. I fly out to Los Angeles at three o'clock."

"Really?" Jonathan's eyes widened in surprise. "Serena cleared that up quicker than I thought she would."

"Yes," Angus nodded. "I still think this country's visa system is a scary thing, but this wasn't as hard as I thought it would be." He held his hand out. "Thanks again."

"It was no problem," Jonathan said. "Enjoy California."

As soon as Angus exited the room, Nicolas let out a derisive snort. Jonathan looked over his shoulder at him. "You good?"

Nicolas nodded, but Jonathan sensed something was wrong. He gestured toward his office, signaling for Nicolas to follow him.

"You'll let me know when lunch arrives?" he asked LaKeisha on the way to his office.

"I ordered Jamaican, by the way," she said. She put her hand up before he could speak. "And, yes, I made sure to order extra beef patties."

Jonathan slapped a hand over his heart. "This is why you can never, ever leave this job."

LaKeisha just stared at him with a bland look that said she only had one nerve left and Jonathan was working on it. He'd been the recipient of that look so many times over the years he saw it in his sleep.

Once in his office, he cleared a couple of thick, leather-covered law books from his desk and motioned for Nicolas to take a seat.

"I've been reading up on Louisiana's forced heirship law," Nicolas said, spreading the file folder open in front of Jonathan. "Do you know this is the only state that has such a thing?"

Jonathan closed the folder. "Forget about this for a minute. I want to talk about what just happened. What's your problem with the guy who just left? Something about him pissed you off."

"It's nothing," Nicolas said. Jonathan tried his best to mimic LaKeisha's bland look. He doubted it was nearly as good as his receptionist's but it did the trick.

Nicolas rolled his eyes, but then said, "I know you can't talk about that guy's case because of attorney/client privilege."

"Actually, he wasn't a client. I was just doing a favor for a fri—for someone," Jonathan corrected. "Do you know him?"

That didn't seem likely, but something about Angus had gotten underneath Nicolas's skin.

"No," he answered. "But I know his type. He's a foreigner, right?"

"Yes."

"A foreigner who had some kind of problem with his visa. And just like that," he snapped his finger, "his problem is solved. He can move about the country however he wants, right?"

"I'm not clear about the specifics, because I directed him to a friend who deals with immigration law, but apparently whatever the issue was with Angus's G-1 visa, it was an easy fix. They were able to clear it up within a matter of days."

"Of course they were," Nicolas said. "That's the way it happens for *some* people."

Jonathan had no idea what was going on, but this wasn't like the mild-mannered kid he'd been mentoring these past couple of months. Nicolas's nostrils flared, the sharp angles of his clenched jaw emphasizing his anger.

"I'm going to ask again," Jonathan said. "What is going on? You can tell me. Maybe I can help."

Nicolas slumped back in his chair, a brooding frown curving his mouth downward. Jonathan had never seen him in this kind of mood.

"It's about my uncle," he finally said.

"Is this your uncle Javier you've mentioned? What about him?" Jonathan waited several beats before he asked again. "Nicolas?"

"His Green Card expired." He sat up in his chair, rested his elbows on his thighs, and hunched his shoulders. "My uncle Javier came here to work construction after Katrina. A lot of people did. Javier probably had an easier time because of my parents—I told you about my parents, right? How they both came here to teach?"

Jonathan nodded. "You said they've been here since the early nineties, right?"

Soon after he'd started here, Nicolas had told Jonathan that his mother taught Spanish and Math at one of the city's private schools, and that his father had been a physics professor at Holy Cross College before he passed away.

"Uncle Javier went through all the proper channels and got a conditional, two year Green Card."

"But he didn't get it renewed after his Green Card expired," Jonathan surmised.

"He got it renewed once, but then stories began to emerge about people being denied and deported. Who knows if it was true or not, but a lot of people who came up here after Katrina decided it was better to take their chances." Nicolas shrugged. "He's been living underground, like a lot of people I know."

"So what's the issue now?"

"My grandmother is sick and Uncle Javier wants to go home to visit. But I'm afraid if he does leave, they won't allow him back into the country," Nicolas said. "I can't lose my uncle, Jonathan. He's the one who helped raise me after my dad died. And I don't want my mom to lose her brother, either. Having Uncle Javier here has been such a blessing for her."

He slapped his hands against his thighs. "And that's why I'm pissed off about it being so simple for that Angus guy."

"Well, they're not entirely the same situation," Jonathan said. He put his hands up before Nicolas could speak. "But I agree that it's unfair what your uncle may potentially face if he leaves, especially with the way things are now. Do you know if he's looked into it?"

"He's too afraid. He's seen enough of his buddies go

home over the years and not be able to reenter. They tell you to go through the proper channels to become a naturalized citizen, but do you have any idea how hard that is?"

He didn't. He didn't even have a working knowledge of immigration law; it just wasn't in his wheelhouse. But during the conversations he'd shared with Nicolas over these past few months, Jonathan had learned enough about the young man's uncle to know that Javier was one of those who'd help to put this city back together again after Hurricane Katrina damn near destroyed it. There was no reason he should be afraid he wouldn't be allowed back into the country after all he'd done to help rebuild New Orleans.

"It's just so damn unfair," Nicolas said. "I wish there was something I could do."

"If it's any consolation, I think you're on the right track," Jonathan said. "Learning how the law works is the first step. The second step is learning how to navigate it. From everything you've shown me over these past few months, you're well on your way to being able to affect change."

"But Uncle Javier needs help *now*." Nicolas stood. "If it's okay, I'm going to leave early today." He pointed to the file folder. "Can we go over this tomorrow?"

Jonathan waved him off. "Don't worry about this."

Nicolas gave him a half-hearted wave before walking out of the office.

Once alone, Jonathan sat back in his chair and rested his folded hands against his lips, contemplating the situation Nicolas's family now found themselves in. He wished there was something he could do. Anything. It *was* unfair. But as things now stood, Jonathan had no idea how to go about making it right.

Chapter Four

MONICA HOLMES WALKED UP to the folding table that had been set up in Toby's living room, hands on her hips. "This is a baby's christening party, why are you people playing cards?"

"Because it's a party," Alex replied. "Doesn't matter what kind. If there's a party going on, that's a good enough reason to play Spades."

Jonathan couldn't help but laugh at the eye-roll Monica directed at her brother-in-law. She perched upon her husband's lap, and Eli automatically wrapped his arm around her waist as he continued to play his hand.

Toby and Sienna had christened their new baby last month, but had postponed the party due to weather. When today rolled around with a forecast for heavy showers yet again, they decided to bring the party inside instead of postponing a second time. Even with a scaled down invitee list that consisted of mostly family, the house was still packed to the brim, which was typical whenever the Holmes family got together.

Last month, before the original party was cancelled,

Jonathan had asked Camille to accompany him. But yesterday, when he'd picked up his phone to extend a second invite, something had stopped him.

Some*thing*? Or some*one*?

Jonathan would rather eat one of the mud pies Toby's kids were making in the backyard than admit Ivana's presence had anything to do with his decision to come to the party solo, but his refusal to acknowledge it didn't make it untrue. He knew she would be here, and his conscience wouldn't allow him to put her in the position they'd experienced the other night, when she'd been force to endure seeing him with another woman.

Not that he'd seen her all that much today. They'd been playing the avoidance game for much of the afternoon. Whenever he stepped into a room, she either wasn't there or she stepped out. But she didn't have to be in the same room with him for Jonathan to feel her presence. He felt her inside his skin, dwelling in his bones. Knowing she was here, in this same space, made him hyperaware of her.

There was something about this day, about this event, that hit him particularly hard.

This could have been them.

When he envisioned his life with Ivana, children had always been part of the equation. *Their* children. He'd wanted a family with her more than he'd wanted anything this universe could provide. He wanted the same joy he'd witnessed in this surrogate family, who had taken him in and treated him as one of their own. The love he saw between Toby and Sienna, Eli and Monica, Alex and Renee —not to mention Toby's cousins, who'd all found love in recent months—it was enviable. He'd wanted that with Ivana. He thought he'd had it with her.

After she left, Jonathan realized he would never get the

one thing he'd most coveted: a child. Not because he was too old. Time wasn't the issue here. It was his heart. He would have to be willing to open his heart and let another woman inside. After the pounding it had received following Ivana's last-minute ditch a week before their wedding, he just wasn't willing to put his heart through that kind of turmoil again.

Instead, he would bask in the gift his best friend had given him. As this new baby's godfather, Jonathan could experience all the fun of spoiling his godson rotten, and then send him back to his mom and dad for them to deal with the consequences.

He tapped out of the card game and went into the kitchen for a bottle of water. He noticed a box of those lemonade-flavored sugar-free drink mixes he usually stole from LaKeisha's top drawer and added one to his bottle.

"Hey, man!" Jonathan turned to find Reid Holmes, Toby's youngest cousin, approaching him. "I was just about to come find you," Reid said. He looked over his shoulder, then, in a whisper, said, "You got a minute?"

Reid nudged his head toward the arched doorway that led to the formal dining room, one of the few rooms in the house that wasn't occupied. Jonathan followed him in there, his sweet tooth instantly salivating at the array of home-made cakes, pies and pralines covered in plastic wrap that cluttered the table.

"What's up?" Jonathan asked.

"So, you know how the fam rented out The Hard Court for my thirtieth birthday a few months ago?" Reid asked. "How much does it cost for something like that?"

"You don't want to know," Jonathan said.

Truth be told, he hadn't charged the Holmeses anything

for renting out his club for Reid's birthday. It had been a very expensive favor he'd given to Harrison, one his law partner still threatened to pay him for. But when Jonathan thought about what the Holmes family had given him all these years, he would do it again in a hot second.

"Why?" he asked. "Is Brooklyn's birthday coming up?"

Reid shook his head. "I'm not looking to throw her a birthday party. Truth be told, The Hard Court isn't really the right venue for what I'm planning." He looked over his shoulder again and then leaned in closer to Jonathan. "Brooklyn was invited to attend this thing for comic book illustrators in Little Rock. It's a pretty big deal. No, it's a *huge* deal. Not many people get in."

"I'm not surprised," Jonathan said. "Your girlfriend is damn good at what she does."

"That's only half of it. Last week we found out she was accepted to one in Chicago, which is even more exclusive than the one in Little Rock," Reid said, pride shining in his eyes. "Anyway, once she's done with both programs, I want to surprise her with a showing of her work, something like you see at the art galleries on Julia Street.

"Alex told me about the place you just bought in that area. It sounds like a cool find. I can't wait to work on it," he interjected. Reid worked as a plumber for his cousin's construction business. "So, do you have an idea of what they charge to rent space in that area for a showing? I figured I'd ask you before I went asking around and got my feelings hurt."

"Let me look into it," Jonathan said. "I haven't met many of my new neighbors, but I can check around, get some prices. Maybe if you hold it on an off day, like a Tuesday or Wednesday night, it won't cost you as much."

Reid held out his hand, bringing Jonathan in for a hug and clamping a solid palm on his back. "Thanks, man. I'll owe you one. Just let me know what I can do."

"Let's see if I can make it happen before we start talking repayment," Jonathan said.

He and Reid rejoined the others, but before Jonathan could reclaim his seat at the card table, Renee used one of the kids' toy megaphones to announce that dinner was ready. The entire clan gathered around the living room with hands joined while Toby's mom, Margo Holmes-Mitchell, led them all in prayer.

After the blessing, a line immediately formed and the twenty or so guests made their way along the buffet. It was crowded with steaming chafing dishes, all filled with jambalaya, mac and cheese, smothered chicken and a half dozen other staples that had Jonathan's mouth watering.

Seconds later, his mouth went bone dry. His luck at avoiding Ivana had finally run out.

She joined the line, with only Ezra Holmes and his fiancée, Mackenna Arnold, separating them. Jonathan told himself not to eavesdrop on their conversation, but how in the hell could he not when she was *right there*?

She asked Mackenna about the state of her mayoral run, then explained that they shared a mutual friend.

"My supervisor in Haiti says she knows you from law school. Patience Edwards?"

"Oh, of course," Mack said. "Patience and I were in the same study group for a couple of years back at Tulane."

"That's what she told me. She was thrilled when she learned you were running for mayor."

"Patience is brilliant. She would have been an amazing lawyer, but her heart was never in it. She's much better suited for the work she's doing now."

"That's kind of what happened with me and my corporate job," Ivana said. "A lot of us found our calling in Haiti. I've never felt more at peace than when I was there."

Jonathan knew he shouldn't allow her words to affect them, but they were like a punch to the gut. How was it that she'd had to leave in order to find peace? Why had it taken her running away from him to make her happy?

He should feel guilty about being upset over her time spent with that relief program. He had no doubt the work she and her colleagues did was vital to the lives of so many in need. But knowing that didn't alleviate his bitterness, or his unquenchable need for answers. He deserved answers, dammit. But it wasn't likely he'd ever get any.

It shouldn't matter. He'd decided a long time ago that this was all water under the bridge. Whether or not Ivana ever took it upon herself to tell him why she'd left, that was up to her. He would be fine either way.

Jonathan swallowed that lie down with a bite of Margo's sweet potato casserole. As he ate his meal, the sense of being watched began to overwhelm him. He glanced to his right and caught Renee and Monica Holmes furtively looking between him and Ivana.

Their curiosity shouldn't come as a surprise. Just about everyone here knew their history. Hell, they all would have been guests at their wedding—if a wedding had taken place.

The delicious food crowding his plate suddenly lost all its flavor. The only thing he had a taste for at the moment was freedom. Freedom from the inquisitive eyes of all these Holmeses, from the suffocating feeling of having his past come back to haunt him in such a public fashion. Freedom from Ivana and all the memories being near her evoked.

He'd give up his favorite pair of Magnanni Cantabria loafers for the chance to walk out that front door at this very second, but doing so would only bring more unwanted attention. Every single person here would know he left because of Ivana.

He would stick it out for another hour. That was doable, wasn't it?

It became a bit easier after Toby fired up the 80-inch in the family room and nearly everyone's focus turned to the NBA game on the television. The game between the New Orleans Pelicans and Houston Rockets was so entertaining, Jonathan even managed to forget about those nosy stares. Basketball had a way of doing that for him. He used to find solace in playing, but these days just getting lost as a spectator brought comfort.

When the buzzer signaling the end of the second quarter rang out, Jonathan attempted for the third time to use the half-bath just off the kitchen, but it was once again occupied. Unable to wait, he went down the hallway toward the bedrooms, and thankfully found the kids' bathroom empty.

As he was exiting it, a bright yellow color caught his eye from just beyond the slightly ajar door of the nursery.

Ivana.

From the moment he'd first spotted her this afternoon, he'd known he would dream about the way the canary yellow skirt she wore today illuminated her pecan-colored skin. He moved closer to the door, his heart catching in his throat at the sight of her standing over the wooden crib. It pissed him off that she still had the ability to take his breath away.

He started to back away, but his feet faltered when she suddenly turned and looked directly at him. Their eyes connected and held for several long moments.

Walk away, a voice whispered to him.

But then, he wasn't a coward who ran away. She was.

Instead of following his first instinct, Jonathan entered the nursery, shoving one hand in his pocket as he slowly made his way to the crib. He maintained his distance, choosing to stand at the foot of the baby's bed instead of next to Ivana on the side.

It felt as if all the air had left the room.

This was the first time they'd been alone together in three years. The significance of that weighed on his skin like a heavy blanket. He tried to think of all the things he'd wanted to say to her for the past three years. All the questions he'd wanted to ask.

But none of it came to him. It was as if it didn't matter now that he found himself alone with this woman he once thought would be his wife.

"Hi," Ivana said in a tentative, hushed voice.

"Hi," Jonathan returned, his voice equally soft. "Needed a breather?"

A slight, sad smile turned up one corner of her mouth. "Just for a minute." She looked down at Jonah and ran her hand over the pale green, gray, and white blanket covering the sleeping baby. "I'm jealous of this little one's ability to sleep with all the noise out there. I can't remember the last time I had such peaceful rest."

Jonathan studied her as she stroked the baby's tiny head, his mind unable to fight the memories that began to assail him.

He'd fallen so damn hard for her. She had been the complete opposite of the kind of women he'd dated in the past, but after taking some time to reflect on it, Jonathan realized that's what had drawn him to her. She complemented him in a way no one else had. She'd taught him to look at the world through a different lens; to see it not as something that he needed to conquer, but as something of beauty meant to be cared for and shared with the rest of humanity.

Ivana Culpepper had changed him for the better. She'd challenged him and motivated him and loved him.

And then she'd run away.

He wanted to know why, dammit! He needed to know what drove her to commit such a selfish, cowardly act.

But if he asked her, she might start to suspect that he wasn't as indifferent to seeing her as he'd let on. He wouldn't give her the satisfaction of knowing what she'd done three years ago still affected him.

"I'm afraid he's going to have Toby's ears," Jonathan said, motioning to his new godchild.

"It won't matter. He'll still be the most precious baby ever," Ivana whispered.

Silence stretched between them, Jonah's soft, contented baby snores the only sound in the room.

Jonathan's skin felt tight, the fabric of his cotton shirt suddenly abrasive against his arms. Being near her again wreaked havoc on his senses. As always, everything was amplified when Ivana was around. Colors appeared brighter, sounds seemed louder; she made his world a more vibrant place. He'd forgotten this feeling. Had forgotten how intoxicating it was to experience even the simplest things with her.

"Want to know something funny?" Ivana continued, that faint smile drifting across her lips once again. "Sienna was the one who never wanted kids. She would always say that she didn't have time for a husband and family, because she was going to take over the business world. Now she's the only one of us with children."

Her observation hit a raw nerve, kindling the burning embers of resentment that Jonathan had tried so hard to bank. They could have had children if she hadn't been such a fucking coward.

Stop it.

There was no point to these recriminations. The only thing such thoughts did was stir up feelings best kept buried.

Stuffing both hands in his pockets, he asked, "So, you've been here for two weeks already?"

She looked up at him, shock widening her gorgeous brown eyes. Guess she didn't think he would call her on it. He hadn't thought he would either. He had no idea where that question had come from.

But now that he'd brought it up, he wanted to know.

"Toby mentioned that the other night," Jonathan continued. "He said you've been back in New Orleans for two weeks. I guess it's nearly three weeks now."

"Umm, yes," she said. "I arrived just before the gala Indina and her brothers held for the start of the foundation they created in their mother's name. It's a wonderful thing they're doing. Diane Holmes was a lovely woman."

Her attempt to change the subject was a clumsy one, but he decided to go along with it.

"You should have come to the gala," Jonathan said. "It was nice."

"I…I did," she said. "I was there."

His brow furrowed. "At the gala?"

She nodded. "Yes. I wore a period costume. Something I borrowed from a friend who rents them out for Mardi Gras."

He thought back to the gala and recalled the tall woman he'd spotted several times. He'd sensed someone watching him throughout the night. His date had even remarked on it, but Jonathan had brushed it off as a weird paranoia.

"Were you wearing a burgundy gown with a big, puffy skirt, and a lace mask over your eyes?"

After a moment, she nodded.

Jonathan saw red.

His anger over the fact that she'd been back in town for two weeks already—and didn't have the courtesy to let the man she was engaged to marry even know—had nothing on the fury surging through him right now. She'd been right there! She'd been in the same damn room with him. After being apart for three years, how could she have been only steps away for an entire evening and not tell him? How in the hell was that supposed to make him feel?

If he'd known she was there that night, nothing would have stopped him from going to her. It wouldn't have mattered that so much time had passed.

"Jonathan," she said his name and his entire being experienced an electric volt. "I know things can never be what... well, what they were. I don't expect them to be. But I'm hoping we can at least be...well...friendly to each other."

He stood there for a moment, contemplating all the things he'd wanted to be to her. All the things he was supposed to be: her lover, her husband, the father of her children. She'd tossed aside everything he'd offered, and now she wanted them to be *friendly*?

Would a friend have avoided him like a damn coward at the gala? Would a friend have ignored him the way she had since she returned to New Orleans? Fuck being her friend.

He took a step closer, lowering his voice for the baby's sake.

"I agreed to help Angus with his issue, but that's as far as my *friendliness* goes. Three years ago I offered you much more than friendship, and you tossed it in my face. I have no desire to be your friend."

She flinched. For a brief second, Jonathan wanted to take the words back. Just the thought of hurting her pierced his chest with an all-consuming ache.

But he suppressed the urge to comfort her. She hadn't cared about how much she'd hurt him three years ago. Maybe it was time she learned how it felt.

IVANA ENTERED through the back door of her mother's house and kicked off her wet shoes, shoving them against the wall. She unwrapped the soaked pashmina from around her shoulders and tried to summon the will to toss it, along with the load of dirty laundry that had been sitting in the hamper since Wednesday, into the washing machine. She opened the washer's lid, but then closed it. She was too dejected to think about laundry right now. After her run-in with Jonathan, it felt as if all the energy had been sapped from her body.

Whatever pinprick of hope she'd held regarding their future withered and died back there in her nephew's nursery. She didn't recognize the man who'd so coldly tossed aside her offer of friendship. The teasing, flirtatious fiancé she'd left behind three years ago had turned into a virtual stranger.

"He hates you," Ivana whispered, the reality of it slamming into her stomach.

She'd thought his indifference stung, but what she'd seen from him today—the coarse rage tightening his jaw, the sheer fury sparking like fire in his eyes—it hurt so much more. If he'd remained indifferent, maybe she could have kept telling herself there was a chance. She could no longer lie to herself after today.

Jonathan Campbell would never love her again. And she had no one to blame but herself.

Ivana walked into the kitchen and stopped at the sight of her mother sitting on one of the high-backed stools at the kitchen island.

"You're back," Ivana said unnecessarily.

"I am," Sylvia replied. "We left Biloxi early, hoping to beat the rain, but it caught up to us just as we crossed the state line. I was going to go to Sienna's but I figured most people had left by the time I got back. Did she have a nice crowd?"

"You know the Holmeses," Ivana said. "They never miss the chance to get together for a party. If I'd known you were back I would have brought you a plate."

"No need to bother." She flicked her hand nonchalantly. "Toby's dropping one off to me on his way back from bringing Margo home. I can count on my son-in-law to take care of me."

Ivana didn't know what to make of her mother's new attitude, especially when it came to Sienna and Toby. Maybe it was the grandchildren she'd always desperately wanted that had mellowed her out.

Sylvia Culpepper wasn't the easiest woman to like. Ivana loved her; she was her mother after all. But to *like* her? That was a different story. On most days, oil and water got along better than she and her mother did. Sylvia had never attempted to see things from Ivana's perspective, and after so many years of trying, Ivana had stopped trying to see things from hers.

But maybe things could be different now. Maybe they could finally get along.

"So, how are you doing after being at the party?" her mother asked.

Ivana shrugged as she walked to the refrigerator and took out the pitcher of sweet iced tea. "I'm fine," she said.

"Fine? Really?"

She turned to find Sylvia staring at her with a raised brow.

"Should I not be fine?" Ivana asked.

"I'm assuming little Jonah's godfather was at the party, so no, I don't expect you to be fine. That couldn't have been easy for you, seeing Jonathan for the first time after all these years. Especially after the way things ended between the two of you."

Ivana froze in the middle of bringing the cup up to her mouth. This was the first time her mother had brought up Jonathan since her return from Haiti.

"Um, actually, this wasn't my first time seeing him since I got back," Ivana said. "I went to his office earlier this week, and Sienna and I went to The Hard Court this past weekend."

Her mother's penciled-in eyebrows arched. "Really? Why were you at his law office?"

"A friend of mine needed help with a legal issue. I went to Jonathan to see if he could get him out of the bind. He did."

"Hmm..." Sylvia murmured. "I'm not surprised. Jonathan's a good man. Unlike that first husband you had."

Ivana nearly spit out the tea she'd just sipped. Years ago, her mother thought Michael Coleman hung the moon, the sun, and the stars. Ivana's decision to divorce him had been just one of the many bones of contention between them. When had her tune changed?

"So, who all came to the christening party?" Sylvia asked.

Ivana shrugged. "I guess you can say it was the typical crowd. Most of the Holmeses, along with a couple of Toby and Sienna's friends."

"Any strangers?"

Ivana frowned. "Strangers?"

Her mother let out an exasperated breath. "Did he have someone with him?" Sylvia asked.

"He? Do you mean Jonathan?"

"Yes, Jonathan. Did he bring a date?"

"No, he was alone."

"Hmm...?"

"What's with you and all the 'hmms'?" Ivana asked.

"Nothing."

Releasing her own sigh, Ivana started for her bedroom.

"Actually, it's *not* nothing," Sylvia called.

Ivana turned to face her. "What was that?"

"It's not nothing," her mother repeated. "I find it interesting that he didn't bring a date with him this time. Whenever I've attended something at Cee Cee and Toby's, Jonathan has always had another woman on his arm."

"Oh wow, Mother! Thanks!" Ivana clamped her hands together in exaggerated excitement. "That makes me feel *so* much better."

"It was meant to. There's a chance he decided not to bring a date because he knew you would be there." Her mother set the cup of coffee she'd been drinking down on the marble countertop. "Of course, it stands to reason that whatever woman he's seeing these days had other plans and couldn't make it."

"Oh, yes, that makes me feel a ton better," she said, inserting as much sarcasm into her voice as she could muster.

"Just trying to look at things from every angle," her mother said. "Whether you believe me or not, I don't want you getting hurt, Ivana."

"Really? When did you start caring about my feelings?"

Sylvia didn't respond. She just stared down her nose with that superior look that always made Ivana feel like a chastised child.

"I'm sorry," Ivana muttered. "That was uncalled for."

"Yes, it was."

Her jaws hurt from the effort it took to keep her mouth shut. She would not reply. She would not.

So much for them getting along.

"I hope you weren't expecting Jonathan to welcome you back with open arms," her mother continued. "You had to have known that he would have moved on by now."

"Of course I wasn't expecting that," Ivana lied. "And what makes you think *I* haven't moved on? I'm the one who left, remember?"

"We all remember that," Sylvia said. She put her hands up. "I just wanted to make sure you weren't setting yourself up for disappointment."

Ivana swallowed down her feelings with the last of her iced tea.

"Don't worry, Mother. I'm not disappointed," she lied. "I was only hoping Jonathan and I could be friends. I'm not pushing him to do anything he doesn't want to do." She shrugged. "Not that it really matters. I'm only here for another month and a half anyway."

She still wasn't sure if that was the case, but Sylvia didn't need to know that. No one did. Not yet.

Ivana left her mother in the kitchen and went into the guest room she'd occupied since coming back home. The lifeless room, with its gray walls, gray furniture and overall coldness was the antithesis of everything she loved, which is probably why it fit Sylvia's style so well.

Her mother had moved out of the house where they'd all grown up, buying this new, bigger house, a few years ago. It made no sense to Ivana. But, then again, a lot of what her mother did had never made sense. She'd never understood Sylvia's obsession with appearances, and her need to impress others. If one of her society friends bought a new car, her mother traded hers in for something bigger and better. If a church member bought new furniture, took an exotic trip, or did something as simple as attending church with a new hat, her mother became obsessed with one-upping them.

Ivana suspected it's why her mother had spent so many years being disappointed in her three daughters. Ivana, Sienna, and their oldest sister, Tosha, had all remained single and childless well into their twenties, while the children of Sylvia's friends had all married and had boatloads of babies. Her mother hated that she was the last to become a grandmother. No doubt it's why she was now Toby's biggest fan. He'd given her the one thing she couldn't buy.

If Ivana had made different choices three years ago, Toby wouldn't be her mother's only son-in-law. Sienna's three kids wouldn't be her only grandchildren.

Self-pity burned like acid in the pit of her stomach.

Ivana fell on top of the duvet, resting her chin on her folded arms. She'd known things would be uncomfortable at Toby and Sienna's. She thought she would be able to handle it, but she hadn't been prepared for that level of scrutiny.

She'd felt like a bug under a microscope, with everyone watching her and Jonathan's every move.

What had they expected? A fight? Some big, emotional scene? Were they all waiting for Jonathan to curse her out in front of the entire crowd?

They should have known better. Jonathan would never do anything like that, no matter how much he disliked a person.

Dislike was probably too kind a word.

It became harder and harder to swallow past the painful lump in her throat. Ivana turned onto her back and fiddled with the ring that had hung on the chain between her breasts for the past three years. She'd considered mailing it back to him so many times, but could never bring herself to do it. After her encounter with him in Jonah's nursery today, wearing Jonathan's ring so close to her heart seemed pointless. She no longer had his heart. He'd made that painfully obvious.

Slipping the chain from around her neck, she let the diamond ring rest in her palm before putting it and the chain in the drawer of the nightstand next to the bed.

Ivana was suddenly hit with a paralyzing sense of grief.

She'd lied when she said she only wanted his friendship. Her most heartfelt fantasy, the one she refused to share with anyone, consisted of Jonathan welcoming her back into his life with the love, joy, and passion they'd once shared. She told Sylvia that she hadn't expected that she and Jonathan would just pick up right where they'd left off, but it's what she'd wanted. It's what she'd prayed for, and dreamed about, and envisioned in the weeks leading up to her return to New Orleans.

But all those things she'd wished for would remain a fantasy. In real life, you didn't leave someone a week before you were set to marry them and expect them to accept you with open arms.

Maybe it was time she finally embraced the fact that what she did to him was unforgivable. It was time she moved on, the way Jonathan had.

Chapter Five

JONATHAN ENDED the call with the Cochran Group's legal counsel, promising a follow-up email regarding the merger they'd discussed. He pushed back from his desk, walked over to the window facing Chartres, and peered down at the street below, searching for the source of the commotion that started a few minutes ago. He frowned in disgust at the group of tourists egging on a drunken guy as he attempted to climb a wrought iron street lamp. Seconds before he opened the window and became one of those crotchety, get off my lawn guys, he noticed a mounted police officer clopping up the street, heading straight for the crowd.

Good. Dealing with sloppy drunks was the price one paid for having an office in the city's most famous neighborhood, but to be that wasted before four in the afternoon? There was no excuse for that.

Jonathan returned to his desk and pulled up the website he'd been reading prior to his last phone call. He scrolled to the center of the page, scanning the text to see if he could find where he'd left off, then decided to print the entire thing and bring it home to read later.

He usually spent his Wednesday evenings at The Hard Court, but he'd sent his club manager a text, letting her know he wouldn't be in tonight. Instead, Jonathan planned to spend the bulk of this evening on the sofa, reading up on this country's jacked up immigration system. He knew the system had issues, but he honestly had no idea the kind of bullshit people had to go through in order to become naturalized citizens.

"Good, you're still here. I thought you'd be out of here by now."

He looked up to find Harrison standing just outside his door.

"Not yet," Jonathan said, motioning for him to come inside. "I just got off the phone with Stewart Jeffrey. I need to send him an email before I can leave."

"Is that the Solar Bright case? No, he's with the Cochran Group," Harrison said, answering his own question. He parked in one of the chairs opposite Jonathan's desk and crossed one leg over his knee. "Did something big go down with the merger? You need help?"

"I've got the Cochran Group covered," Jonathan said. "But there is something else I may need help with. It's about Nicolas."

"What about him? Wait." Harrison held up a hand. "Just so you know, I have no issue with you bringing him on once he finishes up his studies. Better to snap him up before some big firm realizes how smart he is and dangles the sun and moon in front of him. He'll probably have offers coming from everywhere."

"I agree one hundred percent that we should make him

an offer once he graduates," Jonathan said. "But this isn't about work, this is personal."

Knowing he could trust Harrison to keep it confidential, he shared the gist of the conversation he'd had with Nicolas regarding his uncle Javier.

"That's bullshit," Harrison spat once Jonathan finished.

"Agreed. But it's also the law. I've been researching it all day and it's fucking ridiculous the hoops some people have to jump through in order to earn their citizenship. And have you ever taken a look at that citizenship test? I guarantee ninety percent of the people born in this country wouldn't be citizens if they had to pass it. Hell, I didn't know half the answers and I have a degree in political science with a minor in history.

"After hearing what Nicolas's family has endured, it made me curious about how many others have had to face this. Too many," Jonathan said. "What's even more messed up is that so many in this area are the same people who helped to rebuild this city after Katrina. That should count for something, right?"

Harrison nodded. "Those who decide to make a life in a place they helped put back together shouldn't have to claw their way through our immigration system." He shook his head. "But I've got to be honest here, Jonathan. I'm not sure what we can do. Neither of us knows enough about immigration law."

"I know," Jonathan sighed. "I just feel as if I need to do *some*thing."

"You mean *we*. If you're going to take on something this important, I'm going to be right there with you. We just need to figure out what that is exactly."

That attitude was the reason he would never regret joining forces with Harrison Holmes. His partner always had his back. But Jonathan wasn't sure if he was ready to verbalize the idea he'd been mulling over these past few days. There were still so many pieces to it he needed to work through in his head.

Then again, he'd come to count on Harrison's sound input in the years since they'd become partners. Maybe he could help figure out the right path.

"What do you think about providing a sort of project manager for navigating the immigration system?" Jonathan asked. "I keep thinking about what goes into renovating a building. There are all these spokes, and it's the project manager in the center who makes sure the wheel turns smoothly and that nothing falls through the cracks. I'm wondering if there's a way we can provide that person in the center, someone who can guide families through the process."

"It's definitely worth looking into," Harrison said.

"The more I think about it, the more I want to do it. The problem, of course, is that a project like this would require man-hours to both create and run it, and we all have packed calendars."

"Which brings me to the reason I stopped in here in the first place," Harrison said as he shifted in the chair.

His sobering tone gave Jonathan pause. "What's on your mind?"

"Everything has been on pause while we waited for the Delmonico's Machinery acquisition to go through. Now that Bayou Dredging has agreed to cough up the money—"

"Of which Campbell & Holmes will pocket a cool four million, thanks to you."

"You're welcome," Harrison acknowledged with a nod. "But now that we have this huge payday on the horizon, we have some decisions to make. For over a year we've talked about expanding, possibly opening up a second office on the Northshore. But I'm not willing to make that hour-long drive twice a day, several times a week. Not anymore. I made a promise to Willow—and honestly to myself—that I would spend less time at the office and more time with my family. And with the foundation now taking off—"

"I understand," Jonathan said, cutting him off. "I told you weeks ago that I'm good with you taking time off to be with your family. And you absolutely have to be there for the foundation, especially in these first few months. I can hold things down here at the office."

"But this won't be temporary," Harrison said. "My family will *always* be my top priority, and I don't see my time commitment to the foundation lessening anytime soon. And as much as I believe you can handle the caseload a second office will bring, I'm not sure that's the best thing for you, either."

Jonathan's head reared back. "Come again?"

"Look." Harrison held both hands up. "You offered me some unsolicited advice not too long ago. I didn't want to hear it at the time, but it's what I needed to hear. Now it's time I do the same for you. You can't escape the crap in your life that you don't want to deal with by drowning yourself in work. You can try, but it'll eventually catch up with you."

Harrison's words were like a rusty nail scoring an already sore patch of skin.

"I'm not trying to escape anything," Jonathan said. The lift to his partner's brow called him on his bullshit, but Jonathan chose to ignore it. He'd worked too damn hard these past couple of days to put the crap he didn't want to deal with—as Harrison put it—out of his head.

"I'm good," Jonathan emphasized. "You don't have to worry about the practice."

"I'm not worried about the practice. You, on the other hand..."

"You don't have to worry about me either." Jonathan leaned forward and rearranged the stack of *From the desk of...* notepads his sister had bought him as a gift. "That said, I'm actually starting to rethink my position on expanding."

The arch in Harrison's brow became more pronounced.

Jonathan nodded. "I still think we should bring in at least one additional associate, and hold a place for Nicolas when he's done with school. I also think we need to bring in additional help for LaKeisha. She says she doesn't need an assistant, but this is no longer the one man outfit it was when I first hired her.

"As for myself, with this new club I'm planning to open, I'm going to be spread thin already."

"I hadn't even considered that," Harrison remarked.

"I had," Jonathan said. He picked up a letter opener, then dropped it back on the desk. "Instead of taking a portion of that Delmonico's Machinery windfall and expanding to a second office on the Northshore, what do you think about doing more pro bono work with it?"

Harrison pointed at him. "Now *that's* something I can get behind. We could hire someone to fill that project manager role you talked about, but honestly, Jonathan, we can do so much more. This past year of trying to get the Diane Holmes Foundation off the ground has been one hell of an education," Harrison said. "The paperwork regarding compliance and conflicts of interest alone would have cost several thousand in legal fees.

"Our foundation is lucky to have an attorney in the family, but think about all the charities out there that have to spend that kind of money on lawyers instead of using it to help people." He rubbed his hands together. "If we can do anything to alleviate that burden for some, I'm all in."

Harrison pushed up from his chair. "I need to get going. Athens joined the drama club at school and he wants me to come to their practice."

"I guess that sounds fun," Jonathan said with a laugh.

"A bunch of off-key middle schoolers singing show tunes? It's my idea of hell, but it comes with the job of being a dad," Harrison said. He stopped just outside the door. "I'm glad we're on the same page with this pro bono idea. I've been thinking for a while now that we need to start giving back more."

His law partner's excitement fueled his own. At one time Jonathan had earmarked a fifth of his billable hours to providing pro bono legal aid. Helping low-income families fight the city's housing department, offering legal counseling to formerly incarcerated people reentering society. Whatever was needed. But then he'd stopped. Agreeing to mentor Nicolas was the first true act of giving back he'd performed in ages.

When he thought back to the reason he'd allowed his philanthropic work to fall by the wayside, Jonathan could barely stomach the shame. He'd done it to spite Ivana. It didn't matter that she wasn't around to see it, just knowing how it would hurt her was enough for him. He'd wanted to eliminate anything from his life that reminded him of her. And if there was one thing his ex-fiancée had influenced in his life, it was his passion to help others.

Before Ivana, he'd written checks to local charities, donated to toy drives, and sponsored a few families at the women's shelter his sister ran back in Philly. But he'd done it more out of a sense of obligation—or, if he were being honest, out of feeling pressured. Ivana had taught him how to find true joy in serving his community. She'd brought out the very best in him.

When she left, Jonathan had wanted nothing to do with that person she'd helped to create. He'd rejected everything she'd taught him.

He didn't like this person he'd become. He wanted to do better, to *be* better. He wanted to be the man he'd been when he was with Ivana.

Bringing this new pro bono idea to fruition would be a solid first step to reclaiming the charitable spirit he'd once fostered. There were so many people like Javier Moreno, upstanding, hardworking people who had damn sure earned a right to legal citizenship in this country, but were still living in the shadows because of messed up immigration laws. Maybe implementing this project was one way he could get back to being that guy he once was.

IVANA GLANCED up at the clock on the wall behind the register, shocked that only five minutes had passed since the last time she'd looked at it.

She'd spent the past twenty minutes catering to the needs of the sunburned octogenarian who'd been meandering around her mother's souvenir shop. Ivana wasn't sure which would give the woman a hernia first, the overstuffed fanny pack around her waist or the collection of Mardi Gras beads hanging from her neck. She didn't even want to think about how the woman had collected the beads, seeing as the holiday was still several months away.

"What about these ceramic Mardi Gras masks? Are they hand-painted?"

"I don't think—" Ivana started to answer, but her mother cut her off.

"Yes, they are hand-painted," Sylvia said, joining them. "Ninety percent of the items sold here are made by hand. The quality is much better than what you'll find in most of the shops here in the French Quarter."

"Oh, I can see that." The woman lifted a figurine of a jazz quartet from the shelf. "You can tell the stuff in the other shops all come from China."

The bulk of the items Sylvia sold came from Taiwan.

Ivana left the customer in her mother's very capable hands and returned to her spot behind the counter. She slid her Kindle from the cubby underneath the cash register and opened the new Beverly Jenkins she'd downloaded last night.

Foot traffic had been brisk, something she hadn't expected on a Tuesday afternoon. But then Sylvia explained that a huge medical conference was set to kickoff tomorrow at the Ernest N. Morial Convention Center and the deluge of customers finally made sense. The onslaught of souvenir-hunting conference-goers had descended upon them and hadn't let up for hours.

She'd agreed to fill in for the next week while her mother's regular employee, Clarissa, vacationed in Sonoma on a wine-tasting trip with her friends. Despite preparing herself for the mental wear and tear she knew she'd suffer at the hands of Sylvia's persnickety attitude when it came to her shop, Ivana had twice had to stop herself from walking out in a fit of frustration. It had only been two days, but she was ready to beg Clarissa to cut her trip short.

The fact that she and her mother butted heads at every turn was bad enough, but that was nothing new. It was the pure nature of Sylvia's business that had always turned Ivana's stomach.

She shouldn't thumb her nose at her mother's business. After their father died, leaving Sylvia to raise three daughters on her own, this tourist shop had kept a roof over their heads and put food in their bellies. Her mother had worked hard for this business, and deserved kudos for her effort, not condemnation.

It just wasn't Ivana's cup of tea. Which is why she really needed Clarissa to get back here. Or maybe she could contact a temp agency. Was there a place that hired out temporary retail workers?

Who do you think you are? Cinderella's stepsisters?

The words played back in her head like an old commercial from her childhood. It had been Sylvia's favorite saying when any of her daughters complained about having to work in the shop when they were younger. None of them were too good to lend a hand.

And it wasn't as if a bunch of exciting activities populated her day planner. At least filling in at Sylvia's Treasures gave her something to do with her time. She'd found herself climbing the walls after three weeks of getting the rest Patience strongly encouraged her to indulge in. She couldn't handle too many more empty days filled with nothing but Netflix-bingeing.

So what would she do when this short sabbatical was up?

She had some time before deciding whether or not to return to Operation: Heal, but the significance of the choice she would have to eventually make weighed like an anchor in the back of Ivana's mind. Whenever she even thought of going back, a sour sensation settled in the pit of her stomach.

The guilt over her adverse reaction to returning to relief work threatened to suffocate her. She'd devoted so much of her life to helping others, but in the last few months it had become harder and harder to ignore a hard truth she'd spent decades trying to suppress.

She used her relief work as a shield.

She knew she'd been wrong when she left three years ago, but she'd convinced herself it was okay because she was performing noble work. In truth, she'd used her work as an excuse to run away from fears she was too cowardly to face.

"You're such a fraud," Ivana whispered.

The aid she'd provided to those in need over these past three years was laudable, there was no denying that. But she'd gotten something extremely beneficial in return. It had given her a way to assuage her guilt over breaking her promise to Jonathan. Now that there was zero chance for a reconciliation with her former fiancé, her choice of whether or not to return to Operation: Heal should be easy. But it wasn't.

Ivana had no earthly idea what she would do when Angus came back from California, expecting her to hop on a plane with him and return to Haiti. For the first time in years, she longed for the days when she had a plan for her life. She didn't want to go back to being that person who was always the first at the office and the last to leave, but having a bit of direction right now would be nice.

What was she thinking? Being *that* person for so many years had nearly killed her—literally. It wasn't until she found herself in a hospital bed that Ivana finally accepted that she had to make a change in her life.

That fateful hospital stay had been the start of this new life journey she'd been on for the past decade. While she lay in that hospital bed hooked up to monitors, a kindhearted nurse with a sweet, gentle smile had approached her. She'd told Ivana that she had felt a connection to her and was compelled to reach out. Then she'd told her about the work her fellow sisters of the voodoo religion did for the people of New Orleans.

It was the day her life had irrevocably changed.

She'd given up her corporate job and made the decision to devote her life to taking care of others. But it had come at the expense of taking care of herself. The stress of always putting others ahead of herself had taken its toll and led to a level of burnout Ivana wasn't certain she would be able to recover from before it was time to return to Haiti.

She'd visited several of her sisters who still belonged to the cause in these few weeks since she'd return to New Orleans, but warned them that she wouldn't be able to jump back into working with them. They'd understood, of course, and had reassured her that, when she was ready, they would be happy to have her join them in whatever capacity she was able to provide.

Knowing they were so eager to welcome her back into the fold brought such comfort, but Ivana knew she wasn't ready. She wasn't sure if she would ever be ready. But if she didn't go back to Haiti, and she wasn't going to rejoin her voodoo sisters, just what was she going to do with her life?

The question loomed over her like an uncomfortable cloud. The sense of being directionless, of being so unsure of her immediate future, was beyond unsettling. She had some hard, important decisions to make, and the time to make them would be here much sooner than she wanted it to come.

After seeing the tourists out the door, her mother came to stand next to her behind the counter.

"I know it's been a while since you've done this. Do I need to give you a crash course on how to sell?"

"What are you talking about?"

"When that woman asked if that Mardi Gras mask was hand-painted, you were going to tell her no, weren't you?" Sylvia asked, the words soaked in accusation.

"I was going to tell her that I didn't think it was hand-painted, because I didn't think it was."

"The answer is yes, Ivana. It doesn't matter what the customer asks. If it isn't safety-related, the answer is always yes."

"How long have you known me?" she asked her mother. "You know I don't lie."

"It's not lying, it's selling. If you're going to work here while you're in town, then you need to get off that high horse of yours and get with the program."

That sealed it. She would search for Clarrisa's phone number and beg her to come back. It was bad enough she still had more than a week before she would be able to move into her Granny Elise's old house. If she had to spend all day with her mother too, Ivana wasn't sure they would survive it.

Maybe she should look at the bright side. If she and Sylvia killed each other in a murderous rage, at least she wouldn't have to face that hard decision looming ahead.

FOR THE THIRD time in the last three minutes, Jonathan fought the urge to summon an Uber to drive him back to his office. It was only a ten minute walk, but the weather had been a lot nicer when he'd left his law office earlier today. The breeze that blew off the Mississippi River no longer existed, and the morning chill had been replaced with the sticky humidity that tended to hang around New Orleans no matter the time of the year. He'd lived here over a decade, but Jonathan doubted his West Philadelphia born and raised blood would ever get used to this city's weather.

He turned the corner at Royal Street and nearly tripped on the cobblestone sidewalk, his attention misdirected by the sign for Sylvia's Treasures hanging from two chains perpendicular to the entrance of Ivana's mother's French Quarter shop. Even though it was only a few minutes from his law practice, Jonathan had purposely steered clear of this route over the years. Whenever he was forced to take it, he averted his eyes so that he wouldn't see the turquoise sign and be reminded of Ivana. He'd become so adept at avoiding this area that he didn't even have to think about it.

So how had he found himself here today?

It's because he'd been distracted thinking about his meeting with the executives from clean energy powerhouse, Solar Bright. That had to be it. He refused to entertain the notion that it had anything to do with Ivana being back in town.

For one thing, Jonathan knew there was no way in hell she'd be anywhere near her mother's gift shop. Ivana's contentious relationship with Sylvia Culpepper wasn't a secret to anyone who knew the family. She would always say it didn't bother her, but Jonathan could tell that, if given the chance, Ivana would have done just about anything to have a loving, normal mother/daughter relationship with Sylvia.

It had always been his hope to one day help facilitate that, since his one-time future mother-in-law had taken an instant liking to him. But then Jonathan realized just how messed up it was that Sylvia had seemed to like him more than she liked her own daughter.

She'd come to him a week after Ivana left, the day after their scheduled nuptials, and prattled on about how much of a disappointment her flighty daughter had always been and how he'd dodged a bullet by not marrying her. Jonathan had ordered her off his property. On the rare occasion when they encountered each other—usually at family gatherings hosted by Toby and Sienna—they were cordial at best.

Jonathan kept his face forward as he walked passed the shop, but a broad swath of colorful fabric caught his eye. He looked to his left and found himself face-to-face with Ivana, the spotless window the only thing separating them. Her eyes grew wide and her mouth fell open as she stared at him. The bold print of the multicolored scarf tied around her head and hanging along the left side of her body made her luscious brown eyes even more luminous. There was something compelling in those eyes. They urged him to do something he never thought he'd do in a million years.

Without allowing himself time to think about the consequences of his actions, Jonathan walked over to the door, pulled on the brass handle, and entered the shop. He took an immediate left and walked over to Ivana, who remained standing at the window display where she'd been straightening a necklace on a headless, velvet mannequin.

"Well, look who's here!" The sound of Sylvia's voice traveled down Jonathan's spine like Freddy Krueger's nails on a dusty chalkboard. "It's been quite a while since I've seen you."

He turned to the woman who would have been his mother-in-law had his life not taken that drastic, stomach-churning turn. At one time he was more than willing to tolerate Sylvia if it meant having Ivana for a wife. If he could find the tiniest sliver of a silver lining to what happened three years ago, it was that he and this woman were not related.

"Hello, Sylvia. It's been a while," Jonathan greeted her with a light peck on the cheek, as was custom here in the south. "How have you been?"

"Business is steady as always. And, as you see, my prodigal daughter has returned."

He caught the way Ivana's shoulders stiffened.

"Yes, I have," Jonathan said. "I was hoping to steal her away for a bit, if you don't mind. I'm sure it's been a while since she's been to Cafe du Monde for a cafe au lait."

Surprise nearly doubled the size of Ivana's big, brown eyes.

"That's fine with me," Sylvia said. She shielded her mouth with her hand and, in a staged whisper, said, "Keep her as long as you want. She's not the best saleswoman."

Choosing not to acknowledge Sylvia's petty dig at her own damn daughter, Jonathan turned his full attention to Ivana. "Would you like to join me for coffee?"

She hesitated, her wide-eyed stare seeming to ask if he was sure. After a moment, she nodded and pointed toward the register. "Just let me grab my purse."

Jonathan studied her trim frame as she walked to the counter. She wore an ankle-length print dress paired with the tattered jean jacket she'd had for as long as he'd known her. Just seeing the garment brought back unwanted memories. He didn't want to think about the good times they'd had. Those thoughts always led to a dull ache forming in the area of his heart.

Ivana grabbed a small purse with an extra-long strap and what looked to be some kind of tablet or e-reader from behind the counter. When she turned to him, a small but relieved smile graced her features.

"Okay, we can go." She looked over at her mother. "Are you okay closing up by yourself?"

"I've been closing this shop on my own for over thirty years," was Sylvia's reply. "I think I can handle it without your help."

Ivana briefly shut her eyes and pulled in a breath. "I'll see you at home," she called before exiting the door he held open for her.

They'd only walked a few steps before she stopped, backed up against the outside of the building next to her mother's and softly thumped the back of her head against it.

"I want to scream but she would hear me and I don't want to give her the satisfaction." She glanced over at him, her eyes filled with gratitude. "Thank you. I needed out of there."

"Why were you there in the first place?" Jonathan asked. "Your mother's shop is the last place I ever thought I'd find you."

Her luminous eyes went wide with something that looked far too much like hope. "Were you looking for me?"

"No."

Jonathan inwardly cringed at the sharpness of his tone. He hadn't meant to sound so harsh, but he didn't want her thinking he was walking around town looking for her either.

The disappointment that briefly crossed her face made him feel like the worse kind of asshole. He didn't want her getting the wrong idea about his feelings toward her, but he didn't want to be cruel.

"I was at a lunch meeting a couple of blocks over and was walking back to my office," Jonathan explained. "Your mother's shop just so happened to be on the way." He shrugged. "I can't remember the last time I took this route. It's as if fate directed me here to...I don't know...to rescue you. Don't take this the wrong way, Ivana, but your mother is toxic."

"She is." She nodded in agreement. "Thanks again for giving me an excuse to get out of there."

She started to walk away, but Jonathan stopped her.

"Hey," he called. "What about that coffee?"

She turned, confusion blanketing her face. "You were serious? You actually want to have coffee with me?"

It was such a simple question. So why did it feel as if the implications were tantamount to a life-changing decision that could haunt the shit out of him until the end of time?

Or maybe it could just be coffee. Everything didn't have to be so dramatic.

"I invited you, didn't I?" he said.

She stared at him for several moments. Then, with a sad, resigned smile, said, "It's okay, Jonathan. You don't have to follow through."

She once again turned to leave.

"Have coffee with me, Ivana."

The intensity of how much he now wanted that scared him, but the idea of her walking away scared him even more.

"It's just coffee," Jonathan continued, saying it as a reminder to himself more than for her.

He waited several moments while she made up her mind, and was downright terrified at the relief that crashed through him when she finally turned to face him. This was *not* what he should be feeling at the thought of spending the next half hour sharing coffee with the woman who basically ripped his heart out of his chest three years ago. Yet here he was, his bones damn near melting in relief as she came up alongside him.

He would have to take some time to examine this reaction once he was alone again.

Cafe du Monde was packed with tourists, so they ducked into a coffee shop one block over and Jonathan ordered two cafe au laits. He added a boatload of cream and two packets of sugar to Ivana's without thinking about it. It wasn't until she took her first sip, smiled that smile that never failed to knock him to his knees, and said, "Perfect," that Jonathan realized he'd made her coffee just the way she liked it. How had he even remembered?

How could you not?

He used to bring her coffee in bed every morning. It had been the best way to start his day.

Don't think about that.

"So, what are you doing working in Sylvia's shop?" Jonathan asked.

"Besides losing my mind?"

"Besides that," he said.

She shrugged. "I needed something productive to do with myself. I was ordered to take it easy while on my hiatus from Operation: Heal. It isn't a long break in the grand scheme of things, but I can't spend all my time just hanging around."

The fact that she was only here for a couple of months after being away for three years ate at him. Knowing she'd allowed two weeks to pass without even bothering to let him know she was home pissed him off more than Jonathan thought possible. Two whole weeks he'd missed.

But did those two weeks really matter? It wasn't as if they would be together for the next six or eight or however long she remained in New Orleans.

And *that* thought was the one that chafed him more than any other. For her to be so close physically, yet so damn far in every other way, was the hardest thing for him to face.

"What made you leave Haiti after all this time?" Jonathan asked. Of all the questions he wanted to ask, this one seemed the least acerbic.

"My body," she said. "I ended up in the hospital with what my coworkers thought was a heart attack. It turned out to be anxiety and exhaustion."

Jonathan had a hard time swallowing. The mental image of her in a hospital bed somewhere in Haiti made him insane.

"Are you sure that's all it was?" he asked. "Have you been to a hospital since you got back to Louisiana?"

"No, I haven't. And, yes, I'm sure it was just exhaustion. It's been a few months since the hospital stay. I feel much better than I did in the fall, but when a group of relief workers from Guatemala offered to come to Haiti to relieve us, my supervisor advised me to take some time off." She lifted her hands. "So, here I am."

"You need to take care of yourself, Ivana."

She looked at him, those big, vulnerable eyes wreaking havoc on his peace of mind.

"I am," she said in a quiet voice. "I will."

"Really?" Jonathan asked. He hitched his thumb over his shoulder, back in the direction of her mother's shop. "Did I hear you say that you'll see Sylvia at *home*? Does that mean you're staying at her place?"

She released a groan. "Yes. But it's only temporary. I'll be moving into my Granny Elise's house as soon as the current tenant moves out, which is in less than a week and a half, thank God."

"Well, that's something, but I'm not sure working at Sylvia's Treasures is going to help you relax."

"I doubt I'll last much longer at the shop," Ivana said. "I've been in contact with a few of my voodoo sisters working with some of the charities in the city. Miranda's group is renovating a playground in the Seventh Ward. I'm going to wait until they're done with the manual labor before offering my services," she said with a grin.

"What about you?" she asked, stirring her coffee with the little plastic stirrer. "How have you been, Jonathan?"

He refused to be affected by her gorgeous brown eyes or the gentle, solicitous lilt in her voice.

"I've been fine," he answered. "The law practice is going well. Bringing Harrison on as a partner was the smartest move I've ever made."

"And your other venture? Sienna told me about The Hard Court being listed as one of the top clubs in New Orleans."

His brows rose. "So you've been using your sister to keep tabs on me?"

A scarlet hue darkened the crests of her cheeks. "Not in a stalkerish way," she said. "I just...just wanted to know how you were doing."

Jonathan had to work hard to keep his frustration under wraps.

"I guess it's too bad I didn't have someone who could spy for me, huh? There were times during the past three years when it would have been nice to know how you were doing too, Ivana. But when it came to finding any info on you at all, I was shit out of luck."

She looked at him with a chastised expression clouding her features. "I'm sorry," she said.

Jonathan huffed out an irritated snort. What the hell

was he supposed to do with her apology? How did that change the radio silence he'd been forced to endure while she was gone?

"I know you don't want to hear this. You probably don't even care anymore, but I *am* sorry for hurting you," she said, her voice so soft he had to strain to hear it. It was on the tip of his tongue to tell her that she hadn't hurt him, but he couldn't bring himself to voice that lie. They both knew it was untrue.

"Whether you choose to believe me or not, it's up to you. Whether you choose to forgive me or not..." She hunched her shoulders. "That's also up to you."

It wasn't that simple, dammit. The fact that she tried to make it seem that way only pissed him off further. He wouldn't just accept her apology and be done with it. That would be letting her off the hook way too easily.

"I should go," she said.

And there she was, running away again. He should make her stay, demand they finally have this long overdue conversation. But when she stood, Jonathan didn't protest.

"Thanks for the coffee," she said. "And for rescuing me."

And, once again, he watched her walk away from him.

Chapter Six

IVANA SAT behind the wheel of her mother's pearl white Cadillac SRX, her hands wrapped tightly around the buttery smooth leather steering wheel. She usually thumbed her nose at such extravagance, but after three years of riding around in a Jeep with an exterior more rust than metal and seats patched with at least a roll of gray duct tape, Ivana had to admit she could get used to this. If it didn't go against everything she stood for, she would get one for herself.

Of course, she'd have to find the sixty thousand dollars to pay for it first. She still had a nice nest egg from her time in Corporate America, and the alimony her ex-husband had paid up until two years ago, but it wasn't enough to support a lifestyle that included luxury vehicles. The city bus had been her mode of transportation back when she lived here before leaving for Haiti. It would have to do whenever Sylvia wasn't in a sharing mood.

As she continued to sit in the idling SUV, Ivana recognized her stalling for what it was. She'd put this off for several weeks already. If she was going to go through with this whole apology tour thing she had going on, it was time she finally made this stop.

She shifted into Drive and guided the SUV another hundred yards, parking at the curb of the place she'd called home for years. The shotgun-style house she'd shared with her best friend, Lilo, looked as warm and inviting as ever. The exterior had been painted bright new colors since Ivana last saw it. The wooden, clapboard siding a pretty lilac, and the gingerbread trim a soft, sunflower yellow. The coral accents around the window frames and along the roofline added just the right touch of whimsy.

Ivana sucked in a painful breath and got out of the car. Of all the apologies she still had to make, this would be a particularly hard one. Which was why she hadn't been able to coax her coward behind into coming here until now. After the cold reception she'd received from Jonathan, Ivana wasn't sure what to expect from Lilo. Like her fiancé, she'd also abandoned her best friend without giving much of an explanation. There was so much she had to make amends for.

Halfway up the walkway, the screen door opened and Lilo walked out onto the front porch. Ivana's steps stuttered.

"Uhh...hi," Ivana said.

"Hello," Lilo replied, folding her arms over her ample chest. "I was wondering how long it would take for you to show your face."

It felt as though she was trying to swallow a basketball. "I'm sorry it's taken me so long."

Lilo cocked her head to the side. "When you say so 'long,' do you mean the three weeks since you've been back, or the three *years* since you left?"

Ivana hunched her shoulders. "Both?"

"Well, you *should* be sorry," her friend said. Then a

broad smile broke out across her face. "Get your bony behind over here and give me a hug."

Relief washed through Ivana's veins like a flooded river overfilling its banks. She closed the distance between them and stepped into her friend's warm, waiting embrace.

"Thank you...so much," Ivana said, choking on the words.

"For what?" Lilo, who was even taller than Ivana's 5'9" frame, planted a kiss against her temple.

"For not hating me."

Lilo pulled back slightly and looked at her with one brow quirked and a frown on her face. "Who says I don't?" But then she ruined it when she burst out laughing. "Stop it with that foolishness. You know I could never hate you. Come inside. I have someone I want you to meet."

Ivana followed her into the house and a feeling of deep nostalgia immediately overwhelmed her. The exterior may have changed a bit, but inside the walls were still adorned with Lilo's gorgeous photography. Rich, brilliant fabrics and quirky furniture made the house a mishmash of color and fun.

They walked through the living room and into the den. Ivana stopped short at the sight of the little girl who looked to be about three years old sitting in front of the TV.

"Ivana, I'd like you to meet Elsie, my daughter."

Ivana looked from the little girl to Lilo at least three times. "Your what? When did this happen? Wait! Were you pregnant when I left?"

Lilo shook her head. "It's only been four months since we found each other, but she has changed my life in ways I never imagined."

Lilo picked the little girl up, and the child immediately

wrapped her bony legs around her mother's waist. She stared at Ivana with wide, curious eyes.

"Elsie, this is Mommy's friend, Ms. Ivana. Guess what? She used to sleep in your room."

Elsie tucked her head in the crook of Lilo's neck and continued to stare.

"Are you going to say hello?" Lilo asked.

The faint "hello" was barely audible.

"Hello," Ivana said with a smile. "It is so nice to meet you."

Lilo set the child on a large, embroidered pillow on the floor. "Let's let her get back to her television show. She only gets a half-hour of TV time a day, and it's not fair to eat into it. I just made some lavender-honey iced tea. We can have it out on the porch."

Lilo poured their drinks, then they took them out to the painted Adirondack chairs just off to the side of the front door.

"She's precious," Ivana said, tipping her head toward the house. "How old is she?"

"Five."

"Five?" Ivana thought she was pushing it when she thought the little girl was three. "She's so tiny."

"Malnourished as a baby. The doctors are astounded that she doesn't display as many developmental issues as a child who grew up in her conditions usually does, but we still have a long way to go." Lilo sipped her iced tea then set the glass on the small table between them. "I'll tell you all you want to know about Elsie later. Now's the time for you to fess up. I want to know why you left the way you did and why in the *hell* did you not get in touch with me? Not even a postcard, Ivana?"

She'd anticipated these exact questions, yet she still

didn't know how to answer them. She would try. Her friend deserved answers.

"First things first," Ivana said. "I'm sorry. I shouldn't have left the way I did. And not contacting you for three years is unacceptable."

"I agree. If not for your sister, I wouldn't have known you were even alive."

Ivana winced at the hurt in Lilo's voice. "Sienna was the only person back home I kept in contact with," she said.

"I'm waiting for you to get to the why? *Why* did you leave the way you did? And why did you stay gone for so long?"

"The why is...it's complicated."

"That's a Facebook relationship status, not an answer."

"It's the only answer I have." Ivana stretched her arms out. "I cracked under the pressure. That's all I can say. Everything seemed to be happening so rapidly."

"You'd been engaged for nearly two years, Ivana. There was nothing rapid about that."

"I know." She blew out a breath. "But it felt that way." She looked her friend in the eyes and hoped her sincerity came across. "But that had nothing to do with you. I just felt...ashamed. I kept in touch with Sienna because she was the only person I felt I could talk to without being judged." She held up a hand. "That's not entirely true. I knew for a fact that Sienna would most certainly judge me by my actions, but she would also forgive me without question."

"I may not be your sister by blood, but you were always the closest thing I ever had to one," Lilo said. "It cut me up inside that you left the way you did."

Ivana fought through a debilitating ache in her throat as she tried to swallow past the emotion clogging it. What could she possibly say to make up for the horrible way she'd treated someone who'd meant so much to her? She knew it had been cowardly to leave the way she had, but it wasn't until this very moment that she recognized just how astoundingly selfish it had been.

"There's nothing I can say to make up for it," Ivana said. "But I truly am sorry."

Lilo took another sip of her tea and looked out over the flower garden. "How long are you here for?" she asked.

"I'm not entirely sure, but at least six more weeks."

She nodded. "Do you think you can spare some time during these six weeks to get to know Elsie a little better? I've told her a lot about her Auntie Ivana. I'd like her to get to know you."

Ivana's heart filled to the point of nearly bursting.

"Yes," she said, her voice breaking yet again. "I would love that."

"Good, because I need a babysitter next week," Lilo said with a laugh.

Ivana joined in with her. "I'm happy to volunteer."

She'd been so afraid that she'd irreparably damaged her relationship with her best friend. Lilo had every right to send her away without giving her a moment to speak, yet she'd welcomed her back with open arms and a tall glass of lavender-honey iced tea.

But wasn't this what *true* friendship was all about? No matter how big the storm, or who had brought the troubling winds in, true friends were able to weather it.

Maybe a permanent move back home wasn't outside the realm of possibility. She had close friends she could count on to be there for her, even if she didn't necessarily deserve their loyalty. She had family who loved her—although she sometimes questioned that when it came to Sylvia. But her sister and brother-in-law did. So did the Holmes family. She was surrounded by love.

If she could somehow learn to manage the pain she experienced every time she saw Jonathan, maybe she could live in this city of her heart once again.

"TURN AROUND. Just turn. Just turn the hell back."

Jonathan mumbled the words over and over again, but for some reason he'd probably question way too much over the next month, year, lifetime, he continued to drive. Instead of turning around and going back to his office, he pulled up to a parking meter a block away from Sylvia Culpepper's French Quarter shop. He opened the parking app on his phone and bought himself twenty minutes of parking time. What he had to do shouldn't take any longer than that. He wouldn't *allow* it to take any longer than that.

He had a simple yes or no question for Ivana. He would await her simple yes or no answer. And then he would leave.

He still wasn't sure which answer he *wanted* from her. It would no doubt be better for his peace of mind if she answered with a flat out no. If that were the case, he could go back to his office, put her out of his head, and reclaim the life he'd managed to create for himself after she left.

If she answered yes...

Well, that opened up possibilities he didn't want to contemplate right now. Yet, he *needed* her to answer yes. Because this was no longer about him and what would make his life less complicated. It was about helping to right a wrong currently being unleashed upon this city's most vulnerable residents.

Over the past week Jonathan had become obsessed with researching this country's immigration system and trying to come up with a way to help families like Nicolas's. There were so many confounding layers to it. Something *had* to be done.

But he couldn't do it alone. He had a law practice to run, with long-standing clients who paid him extremely handsome retainers and expected him to handle their work in a timely manner. He was also at the helm of one very successful nightclub, and trying to get another still in its infancy stages off the ground.

But like a dog with a damn bone, Jonathan could not let this go. The deeper he delved into Javier Moreno's situation, the more aware he became of the problem so many of the hardworking people in this community faced. And it sickened him.

On any given day, Jonathan would admit to being an arrogant bastard, but even *he* wasn't cocky enough to think he knew enough to tackle this issue. There were a number of brilliant legal experts out there, like Serena Dayton, who had been navigating the murky waters of immigration law for years. He would leave the heavy lifting to the professionals.

But that didn't mean he had to sit around twiddling his thumbs. The more he researched, the more issues he'd discovered *outside* of the courtroom that those seeking citizenship must face. He could figure out a way to assist people with those issues. Well, Campbell & Holmes could figure it out, if they hired an intelligent temporary employee with a penchant for wanting to help people.

He stared at the turquoise sign hanging perpendicular above the door.

"There has to be someone else who can do this," Jonathan muttered.

But he knew there wasn't another soul on this earth who would attack this matter with the heart, determination and compassion that Ivana would. Her sole purpose in life was to fight for those in need of help. If Campbell & Holmes provided her with the tools and support she needed, Ivana would come up with a program that could potentially aid dozens, if not hundreds, of hardworking, dedicated people who were just trying to make a better life for themselves and their families. He had to put aside his personal feelings. This was too important to allow anything to get in the way of it.

He opened the door, the bell above it signaling his arrival.

If anyone had bet him that he would enter Sylvia Culpepper's French Quarter tourist shop twice within a two-day timeframe, Jonathan would have been on the losing end of that bet. That's why he didn't gamble. Because two days ago, just the thought of doing what he was about to do would have had him packing his bags and leaving town.

A short woman with a curly, two-inch afro and bright pink glasses smiled at him from behind the counter. "Welcome to Sylvia's Treasures, may I help you?"

"I'm looking for Ivana," Jonathan said.

"Are you now?"

He pivoted. He hadn't noticed Sylvia over in the far right corner of the store when he'd entered.

"Hello, Sylvia," Jonathan said.

"So, are you and Ivana a thing again?" she asked.

"I just need to speak with her," Jonathan said. "It's pertaining to my law practice."

"Is this about that little redheaded friend she brought

back with her from Haiti? I thought he would be gone by now." She sucked her teeth. "Personally, I think she needs to crawl to you on her hands and knees and beg you to take her back."

Most men would be flattered by a mother-in-law who did her best to ingratiate herself to them, but not Jonathan. When he compared the way Sylvia treated him to the way she treated her own daughter, it did nothing but piss him off.

"Is Ivana in the back?" he asked, gesturing with his head toward the storeroom.

"She's at Sienna's," Sylvia said before turning back to the scarves she'd been hanging on a circular rack.

"Thank you." He immediately left the store. He had no desire to spend any more time with Sylvia Culpepper than necessary.

He drove straight to Sienna and Toby's, but once there, discovered that no one was home. He called Toby, who was currently in Houston auditioning opening acts for Aria Jordan's upcoming European concert tour. The last Toby had heard from Sienna, she and Ivana were enjoying a brunch of homemade Grand Marnier French toast and mimosas.

Jonathan doubted they were both passed out drunk from one too many mimosas, which meant they'd taken off somewhere. He texted Sienna, but didn't receive a reply.

A sensation that felt both heavy and light tumbled around in his gut as he pulled up Ivana's number in his phone's contacts list. He'd stored it under *Indigo*, the title of one of her favorite novels, because at one time he couldn't bear to even see Ivana's name. Yet, he couldn't bring himself to delete her from his phone either.

He started to text her, but then stopped. He didn't even know if this was still her correct number.

Jonathan pressed the back of his head against the headrest and closed his eyes tight, disgust and disbelief plunging him into an instant state of turmoil. This was the woman he'd planned to spend the rest of his life with. How had they gotten to the point where he didn't even know her fucking phone number?

Because she'd left him, that's how. He'd been prepared to give her the world, and she'd tossed it in his face with her last-minute ditch.

Familiar pain sliced across his chest.

God, what was he doing here? How had he thought for even a minute that he could invite Ivana into his world again? Even if it was just temporary, he would be a fool to purposely put himself through that kind of pain.

Jonathan revved up the ignition and shifted it into reverse. But just as he started to back out of Toby's driveway, a taupe SUV turned in, pulling up alongside his Tesla. Ivana's eyes widened as she looked at him from the passenger seat.

"Well, hell," Jonathan muttered. If he'd had his revelation just two minutes earlier he would have made a clean getaway.

He shut the car off and got out. Ivana remained in the SUV, but Sienna had already rounded the front bumper by the time Jonathan reached her.

"Hey," she greeted, wrapping him up in a quick hug. "What are you doing here on a Thursday afternoon?"

"Did you get my text?" Jonathan asked.

She looked down at her phone. "I had it on 'Do Not Disturb' while we were in the movies, so Toby and the kids' daycare are the only numbers that could get through. Sorry about that."

"The movies? Who goes to the movies on a Thursday afternoon?"

"Someone who's about to return to work after months of maternity leave," she said with a laugh. "I'm trying to squeeze in all the things I won't be able to do once I'm back at the nine-to-five. So, what's up?"

The passenger side door opened and Ivana climbed down from the SUV's high front seat.

"I...umm...needed to speak with Ivana," Jonathan said.

Sienna's brows spiked, her eyes wide and curious. "Really? Well, okay, then," she said. "I'll just leave you two alone while I get this ice cream into the freezer."

Apprehension radiated from Ivana as she approached him, her brown eyes teeming with unease.

"You need to speak with me?" she asked.

Jonathan knew her well enough to not be fooled by her taciturn demeanor. She put on a brave, reserved front, but he heard the tremulous quiver in her voice.

"Yes, I wanted to talk to you about something." As opposed to talking to her about nothing? Shit, he needed to get it together. "I have a job offer for you," he said, deciding to get right to the heart of the matter.

Her head jerked back in surprise.

"It's not a typical job," he continued. Jonathan held his hands up. "Let me start over." He rested his backside against Sienna's SUV and tucked his hands in his pockets. "A couple of days ago, an issue came to my attention and I haven't been able to get it out of my head. In a roundabout way, you and your friend Angus are the reason it landed on my radar."

"What are you talking about, Jonathan?"

Without going into too much detail, he gave her a brief overview of the situation with Nicolas's uncle.

"This is ten times more complicated than Angus's dilemma, so I didn't even attempt to help Javier with any of the legal issues. There are lawyers far more qualified to do that than I am. But there are other things that can benefit those going through the immigration process. I want to design a program to aid those seeking citizenship—specifically those who came here to help rebuild the city after Hurricane Katrina and are now living in the shadows because they're afraid they'll be deported if they speak up."

She shook her head. "I know less about the immigration system than you do. That's why I came to you with Angus's problem in the first place."

"You were under an extreme time crunch with Angus's problem." He paused. "Actually, Javier Moreno is under a time crunch too, but I'm hoping the same friend who helped Angus will be able to help Javier.

"What I'd like *you* to do is research ways to help those who have been here for over a decade, and who want and deserve to stay, but don't know how to go about making that happen. There are organizations out there doing great work, but from what I see there are still gaps. I want to find better ways to fill in those gaps."

"So, why me?"

"Because you've spent your adult life helping people. I don't have time to create the kind of program I'm hoping to build. I need someone who's smart, someone who would approach this with the kind of compassion and understanding people in this situation need." He paused for a moment and swallowed deeply before he continued. "I need *you*, Ivana.

"To set up this program," he quickly added. He needed

to make sure she didn't read anything more into his offer. This was temporary employment, nothing more.

Jonathan pushed up from where he'd been leaning on the car. "It's better than working in your mother's tourist shop. You'll be doing something worthwhile that has the potential to help hundreds of people."

"I—" She folded her arms over her front, cradling her elbows in her palms.

"I know you're leaving," Jonathan said before she could bring it up as a concern. "Once the program is in place, I'll look into hiring someone to handle the day-to-day operations. I just need to have something in place for them to run before I hire them to actually run it."

Jonathan watched as the emotions played across her face. Curiosity, apprehension and finally, resignation.

With sadness in her eyes, she shook her head and said, "I'm not sure this is a good idea."

Even though he'd expected it—had prepared for it—her rejection still stung, its after effects leaving a bitter, familiar taste in his mouth. He'd been on the receiving end of her rejection before; he should be used to it.

"I just—" she started, but he cut her off.

"No. That's okay," Jonathan said. "No explanation necessary. You're right. I'll find someone else to do it."

"Jonathan—"

He pushed away from the SUV and got into his car, slamming the door of the $100,000 vehicle before the automatic door-closing system could engage. He shoved his foot against the break, turning the car on, and backed out of the driveway. He refused to look at her.

This was for the best. He didn't know what the hell had driven him to come here in the first place.

FOR THE SECOND time since she'd returned to New Orleans, Ivana found herself in the well-appointed parlor that served as the lobby for the Law Offices of Campbell & Holmes. When she'd left three years ago, it had only been Campbell. Sienna told her about Jonathan bringing Toby's cousin in as a second associate, but she didn't realize Harrison was a partner until Jonathan mentioned it over coffee.

She'd been so nervous when she was here with Angus that she hadn't taken the time to observe all the changes here in the parlor. The cherry wood chairs and coffee table had been replaced with a lighter wood that helped to brighten the space. Crowded bookcases no longer lined the walls. Instead, framed artwork hung in their place. It made the room seem twice as large.

A bittersweet smile stole over her lips at the sight of the Tiffany lamp on the small table tucked into a corner. The rich, vibrantly colored stained glass dragonflies and daffodils were as beautiful today as they were the day she'd picked it out at the auction they'd attended in Dallas. Jonathan had gotten rid of so many of the things they'd bought together, seeing the lamp triggered a poignant ache deep in her chest.

"Ms. Culpepper?"

Ivana sat up straight at the receptionist's cool voice. "Yes, LaKeisha?"

"Mr. Campbell can see you now. His next appointment is due to arrive in ten minutes, so please keep that in mind."

"I will. Thank you," Ivana said, quickly walking past the receptionist's desk. She wasn't all that surprised at the woman's chilly tone. LaKeisha had always been loyal to Jonathan. Much more loyal to him than his former fiancée.

She sucked in a fortifying breath as she approached his office, quickly releasing it before she knocked on the door.

"Come in."

She found him sitting behind his desk, his shirt sleeves rolled up to the middle of his forearms. Even though it had been more than a decade since he'd played professional basketball, he still had that lean, athletic build. Ivana wondered how different things would be if he were still a basketball player.

They would have eventually met—his profession wouldn't have changed his relationship with Toby. But her aversion to those who earned obscene amounts of money would have compelled her to keep her distance. She doubted she would have given Jonathan more than a passing glance if he'd remained an NBA star.

Ivana mentally chastised herself. She'd vowed to work on her prejudice against the rich after discovering just how many athletes, movie stars, singers and business owners contributed to the work they did in Haiti, many of them without ever making their donations known to the public.

Jonathan would have been one of those celebrities. Years ago, she'd accused him of being a selfish lawyer and nightclub owner, only to discover that he generously gave to numerous causes. That giving nature of his was the reason she found herself in his office today.

"LaKeisha said you could see me now?" Ivana said.

He looked up from whatever he'd been working on, his eyes rounding with surprise, as if he hadn't been expecting her.

"Yes. I'm sorry, come in." He shook his head and

motioned for her to take a seat. "What can I do for you, Ivana?"

His brisk, businesslike tone was not unexpected. Still, it stung.

"I may have responded a bit too abruptly to your proposal yesterday," Ivana said as she sat in one of two chairs facing his desk. "After taking some time to think about it, I recognize just how essential the program you're seeking to put in place is for so many people in this city." She folded her hands on her crossed knee. "If the offer still stands, I'd like to take you up on it."

Jonathan sat back in his chair. He tapped the fountain pen he held against his palm. "Are you sure about that?"

She nodded. "I am."

"What brought about this one-eighty? Just yesterday you said it wasn't a good idea."

"It's not that the *idea* isn't good—"

"No, it's just the idea of working with me that you don't like. That's it, isn't it?" He huffed out a humorless laugh, tossing the pen on the desk and leaning forward. "Is that your problem, Ivana? Working with me?"

"Well, yes. No. Goodness, Jonathan." She shook her head. "I assumed *you* would have a problem working with *me*. You've made your feelings known. I didn't want to cause any further harm than I have already by coming back here."

He started to speak then stopped, his jaw tight with what she could only assume was anger.

"Why don't you let me decide what I can or can't handle when it comes to you being back," he said.

As much as she'd prepared herself for his ire, being on the receiving end of it cut through her like a sword.

"I don't know what it is you want from me, Jonathan."

"I told you what I wanted from you yesterday. Your response was to tell me that it wasn't a good idea."

There was no getting through to him. That was more than obvious. Ivana braced her hands on the chair's spindly arms, preparing to stand. But then she stopped.

If she walked out of here right now, that would be the end of it, the proverbial nail in the coffin of any involvement she could ever hope to have with him. There would be no chance to regain some semblance of a friendship. She wasn't ready to close that door just yet.

"Jonathan, you have every right to be angry. I tried to apologize for what I did, because that's all I can do at this point." She lifted her shoulders in a hapless shrug. "If you want to go the rest of your life hating me, there's nothing I can do about that. No one would blame you for feeling the way you do, least of all me," she said, despising the way her voice cracked.

She should stop. The futility in trying to reach past his anger was evident. But now that she held this captive audience of one, she wanted to say everything that needed to be said.

And then, if he asked, she would walk out of here and never return.

"I was wrong to leave the way I did three years ago," Ivana said. "I regret it more than I can possibly describe. When I decided to return to New Orleans, it was with the hope that I could earn your forgiveness, even though I have no right to it."

A muscle twitched in his jaw. She'd never seen him so angry, and this was after three years. She didn't want to imagine the rage he must have felt in the days just after she left for Haiti.

"I have no right to your forgiveness," Ivana repeated. "If

it would make you feel better to tell me each and every day how much you hate me, then do it. You would be justified. If you want to flaunt your women in my face—" She paused. Swallowed. "That's fine, too. Go right ahead. It's nothing less than I deserve."

She sat up in her chair, straightening her spine. "But it doesn't change the fact that what you're proposing to do with this new program is important and necessary for thousands living in this city, and I would like the chance to help you build it. I'll learn how to deal with the...with the rest."

Her words hung in the air, a dense weight on her skin. Jonathan continued to stare at her with eyes so intense Ivana could feel herself shrinking under the scrutiny.

"I don't hate you, Ivana." The words were spoken so softly she barely heard them. "I don't—" He shook his head, his gaze now bouncing from one object to another. Anywhere but at her. "I don't want to feel anything when it comes to you."

He didn't *want* to feel anything when it came to her? Did that mean that he felt *some*thing?

It was on the tip of her tongue to ask him to clarify his words, but Ivana doggedly fought it. If his answer wasn't what she wanted to hear, it would hurt worse than not knowing. She'd endured enough emotional turmoil for the day.

"What about the position?" she asked instead. "Is it still open?"

It had been less than twenty-four hours since he'd first approached her with his idea. She doubted he'd found someone else for the job that quickly.

But he remained silent. Was he wondering whether or not it was worth it to have her around? What if he couldn't find anyone else for the job? Would he just abandon it? The thought of him deciding not to pursue something she could tell meant so much to him simply because he couldn't stomach having her around made Ivana physically ill.

"I'll ask LaKeisha to get the office down the hall ready for you," he finally said, jiggling the computer mouse and directing his attention to the monitor on his desk. "It's where I plan to place our new associate, but we won't be hiring anyone in that position for another few months." He looked at her, one brow cocked. "You'll be back in Haiti by then."

Ivana managed not to flinch at the hint of accusation that laced his statement.

"Do you have a framework for the program you'd like to set up?" she asked.

He clicked the mouse several times more, then once again reclined in his chair. "You'll have full reign here. Go wherever the research takes you."

His phone buzzed and LaKeisha's voice came through the line. "Your two o'clock is here."

"I guess that's my cue to leave," Ivana said.

She stood. So did he.

Jonathan rounded his desk, but he didn't make any move to touch her. He simply waited while she gathered her purse, then he walked with her to the door and out of his office.

He spoke to LaKeisha. "Ms. Culpepper will be doing some contract work starting..." He looked to Ivana. "Is tomorrow too soon?"

She shook her head. "No. That's fine."

"Starting tomorrow," Jonathan said.

With that, he turned to greet his two o'clock appointment. The handsome, astutely dressed South Asian man wearing a Sikh turban nodded at Ivana before shaking Jonathan's hand and following him into his office.

She stared at the closed door, wondering if she'd made a grave mistake in offering to work here. She jumped when LaKeisha cleared her throat.

"Will you need anything specific for this job I had no idea even existed at Campbell & Holmes?"

This time Ivana did flinch. She understood LaKeisha's frosty attitude. She was only trying to protect the man she'd worked for all these years from being burned again. It was admirable. But it still hurt. Ivana wouldn't describe their past relationship as particularly close, but at one time, she'd considered LaKeisha Lawrence a friend.

"Just a computer and supplies for taking notes," Ivana said. "I'll bring whatever else I need."

LaKeisha nodded. "It will be ready tomorrow." She returned her attention to her computer monitor.

She'd been dismissed.

Swallowing past the ache in her throat, Ivana shouldered her crocheted hobo bag and left.

Chapter Seven

JONATHAN FLIPPED through the pages of the leather-bound tome he'd taken from the built-in bookcase behind his desk, his frustration growing as he continued to come up empty-handed. He clearly remembered making notes in the margins of a law book that dealt specifically with the state's Usufruct and Right of Habitation law. He needed to find those damn notes.

He pulled another off the shelf and paged through it, but then stopped and shut the book. The usufruct law wouldn't be in any of these. It fell under the Napoleonic Code, which was unique to Louisiana's civil law.

"Shit," he whispered as he slid the book back into place, rested his folded hands on the shelf and leaned his forehead against them.

All of the books on the Napoleonic Code were kept in their small library, which meant he would have to leave this office in order to search for it. Which meant he would possibly see *her*.

It was a damn shame that a grown-ass man would sequester himself in his own office to avoid running into a woman he'd *asked* to work here, but that's exactly what he'd done for much of this week. What in the hell had he been thinking? Inviting Ivana to work at Campbell & Holmes was like a diabetic purposely choosing to work in a bakery. Nothing good could come from all that temptation.

He was disappointed in himself—disappointed and frustrated. And surprised. He'd spent the past three years building up a thick crust around his heart, yet after just one week of being near her every day, Jonathan found himself on the precipice of tumbling right back in love with her.

No. No, he wasn't. There was absolutely *zero* chance of him doing anything that even *remotely* resembled falling back in love with Ivana Culpepper.

So why was he holed up in this office, afraid to walk around his own damn law practice?

He pushed away from the bookcase and attempted to bring the butterflies in his stomach under control as he strode toward the door. Butterflies. The woman had butter-flies floating around his stomach.

The moment Jonathan stepped into the hallway, he heard her musical laugh drifting from the kitchen/break room. He shut his eyes tight, fighting off the wave of longing that threatened to pummel him. God, how was he supposed to function with her here?

She'd already charmed her way back into LaKeisha's good graces. The two had taken their lunch break together yesterday, sharing a platter of hummus with all the fixings from his receptionist's favorite lunch spot while talking about some British TV show they were both binge-watch-ing. Jonathan had wanted to make a crack about misplaced loyalties, but this wasn't about him versus Ivana. *He* was the reason she was here. How could he be upset that she was getting along with the staff?

The whiff of whatever spicy deliciousness they were having for lunch reminded him that he still hadn't eaten.

He'd turned down two invitations to lunch this week, the most recent just a few hours ago. Marlee Jacobs, a former public defender he'd dated last year, had asked him to join her at Maspero's for a goodbye lunch before she left for a new position in Birmingham. Jonathan didn't want to look too deeply into the reasons why he'd turned her down.

As if you don't know.

He knew exactly why he'd fed Marlee the lame excuse of having too much on his plate and needing to work through lunch. When he considered sitting in a restaurant with another woman across from him, all he could think about was the vulnerable, forlorn look he saw in Ivana's eyes every time he caught her staring at him the night she came to The Hard Court.

Her hurt feelings were no longer his concern. Yet, Jonathan realized that he just couldn't do it. He could not knowingly cause her pain, no matter how much pain she'd caused him.

For reasons he couldn't explain, Jonathan walked past their office library and into the employee break room. What happened to avoiding her?

"There you are," LaKeisha greeted. "I was wondering if you were ever going to come up for air. Are you still working on that case between those two .brothers?" She looked over at Ivana. "Two filthy rich brothers out in Ascension Parish are fighting over land that doesn't belong to either one of them. It's a mess."

"The problem is, they both have a leg to stand on because of an obscure Louisiana law," Jonathan said.

"I believe Nicolas left the information you asked him to research on his desk. I'll get it after I'm done with my lunch," LaKeisha said. She gestured to her bowl. "You should try some of this. Ivana made it. I've never had true Haitian food before and I think I'm in love. It's called mayi...what?"

"Mayi Moulen Kole ak Legim," Ivana said, the words rolling off her tongue like a song.

"Yeah, what she said. It's some kind of stew with beans and cornmeal that has me ready to turn vegetarian."

The antique doorbell at the front entrance chimed, followed by the "smart" doorbell's computerized voice alerting them to a visitor at the door.

"Let me get that. It's probably the courier dropping off the package from D'Amico and Associates," LaKeisha said.

"I can—" Jonathan said, but she'd already rushed out of the break room. She'd always been too damn efficient.

And just like that, he found himself alone with Ivana for the first time this week.

Needing to occupy his hands, Jonathan walked over to the coffee machine and popped in a pod. As he waited for the machine to brew the coffee he didn't even feel like drinking, he rested his backside against the counter and decided to behave like a normal human being who was capable of making small talk with another human being.

"How is the work going so far?" he asked.

She dabbed at the edges of her mouth with her paper napkin before speaking.

"Good." She nodded. "At least I think it's good so far. I've been researching what some of the organizations in other states are doing. No use in us reinventing the wheel, right?"

Her use of the word "us" nearly killed him. Now that she was working at Campbell & Holmes, they were an "us" in a way, but not in the way he'd always pictured. *That* us consisted of the two of them as husband and wife. As mother and father to the children they created together. As soulmates.

He blocked the images from his mind as he focused on her words. She shared her current approach to developing the program he'd hired her to create, explaining how she'd spent the week delving into the various ways in which New Orleans's immigrant population was not being served.

"I came up with a prioritized list based on matters of importance. Nicolas agrees that the issues I plan to tackle first are the most urgent," she said. "He is fully onboard."

The only thing that surpassed Nicolas's gratitude when Jonathan told him about the program, was the young law student's enthusiasm to work with Ivana on building it. Not that Jonathan could blame him. Even now, as he observed her passionate, detailed explanation about some organization she'd run across while researching, Jonathan couldn't help but smile. Her eyes lit up with excitement.

"What?" she asked, her bemused tone communicating her confusion.

"Nothing." He shook his head. "It's just...look at you. All it takes is a worthy cause, and you're right there, ready to take it on." He sobered as poignant memories assailed him, reminding him of why he'd fallen so hard for her the first time. "Never change, Ivana. The world needs more people like you in it."

That guarded, almost fragile look entered her eyes, as if she wasn't sure how to process his simple compliment.

"Thank you," she answered after a few moments, her smile both sweet and demure, and—God, help him—sexier than it had a right to be.

Myriad emotions reverberated throughout his being as

he studied her features, but the one that struck the deepest chord was the longing that grabbed hold of him.

He felt it happening. He could feel himself falling for her again.

No. He would not allow her to climb so easily back into his heart after the way she'd broken it so completely three years ago.

Clearing his throat, Jonathan pushed away from the counter and dumped the full mug of coffee in the sink.

"I need to get back to work," he said.

"Yes. Yes, of course," she said, blinking several times as if startled. She covered the container of leftover soup with a plastic lid and stood. "Would you like to see what I've put together so far?"

"That isn't necessary."

The words rushed forth before he had the chance to consider how they would sound to Ivana's ears. Shit, he didn't want her to think he had no interest in the project now that he'd handed it off to her.

"You can send it in an email," he added, tempering his tone. "I'll look it over when I have some free time."

She paused, then after a brief nod, said, "You'll have a summary by the afternoon." There was a hint of austerity to her voice that hadn't been there a minute ago.

He should probably say something. Maybe apologize for his harshness?

Or maybe he should just stick to his original plan and try to avoid these awkward encounters with her altogether.

Jonathan headed for the door, but stopped when Ivana called his name. He counted to three before turning to face her.

"Yes?" he asked.

She stood with her hands folded in front of her, a pensive expression distorting her lovely features.

"I'm not sure I can continue to do this," she stated.

He frowned, taken aback. "I thought you said the work was going well?"

"I'm not talking about the work, I'm talking about this." She gestured to the space between them. "It feels as if I'm walking on eggshells when I'm around you and I...I don't want to feel this way."

Jonathan slipped a hand in his pocket as he took a step toward her.

"Are you saying you want to quit?" he asked, apprehension tightening his chest.

"No." She shook her head. "No, I just—" She released a frustrated breath. "Forget I said anything."

"Ivana—"

"I'll get back to work."

She tried to brush past him, but Jonathan caught her by the wrist. Her eyes shifted from his face to where he held her, but he didn't let go.

"When has walking away ever solved anything between us, Ivana?"

She flinched. Jonathan hadn't meant for the words to sound like an accusation, but he could tell that's how she'd interpreted them.

"I don't want you to feel uncomfortable while working here," he explained. "Talk to me. Maybe we can figure something out."

She gave a brief nod, and Jonathan let go of her wrist.

She backed up, assuming the pose he'd previously held, clasping her hands in front of her as she leaned against the counter.

"I knew this would be difficult," she started. "I was so

sure I could handle it, but I don't know." She pressed her lips together. "Being here, seeing you every day—it's a constant reminder of one of the biggest mistakes I've ever made."

He studied her for a moment. "Which do you consider the mistake?" he asked, his throat suddenly tight. "Leaving me, or being with me in the first place?"

Her delicate, regretful smile tore at his heart. "You know better than to ask that question," she whispered.

He fought the urge to reach for her, to go to her. He wanted to forget the past three years had ever happened and just go back to loving her. His world was a richer, happier place when he let himself love her.

But he couldn't do that. Just the idea of leaving his heart so exposed scared the hell out of him.

"But, once again, I'm reminded that this isn't about me, or about us," Ivana said with exaggerated buoyancy, her smile overly bright, as if she was trying extra hard to hold on to it. "This is about those thousands of people who need our help."

"It is," he said with a nod. "So, how do you propose we get past this...awkwardness?"

She lifted her shoulders. "You didn't respond all that well the first time I suggested this, but I think it would help if we tried to be friends?"

"This again." He pinched the bridge of his nose and huffed out a derisive snort.

"Would it really be that much of a hardship, Jonathan?"

He arched a brow. "You do realize you were never my friend, don't you?" She opened her mouth to protest, but he stopped her. "It's the truth. You hated me from the first day you met me."

"Hate is a very strong word," she said, lifting that regal nose in the air. "Disliked, maybe?"

"Intensely disliked," Jonathan said. His gaze dropped to the delicate hollow at the base of her throat. Memories of how he would caress that spot with his tongue ravaged him, reminding him of a time when he couldn't get enough of this woman. "But that dislike quickly turned to lust. And then to love."

He studied her reaction, observing the way her chest rose and fell with her shallow breaths.

"Friendship?" He shook his head. "The concept is too bland, too unexciting. I'm not sure it could ever work for us, Ivana."

Palpable awareness pulsed between them as she searched his face, her eyes locking with his. His heart banged against his chest, the sudden need to go to her overwhelming him.

"But we can try," Jonathan said, taking a step back. He cleared his throat. "I'm willing to go along with it if you think it will make this easier. Send along that summary when you have a chance."

He left the break room and took off toward his office, his hands shaking so badly he had to stuff them in his pockets to avoid LaKeisha possibly seeing the tremble and asking questions. He made it to his office and closed the door behind him, resting his head back against the smooth wood.

"Her *friend*," Jonathan whispered. "Yeah, good luck with that."

IVANA READ over the same paragraph three times before recognizing the futility in pretending to work. Her output had been dismal since just after ten o'clock this morning, when she'd approached the slightly ajar door to Jonathan's office and overheard him on the phone.

It wasn't the fact that he'd been on the phone with another woman that had caused this particular knot to form in her stomach—he spoke with women all day long. It was the ease and familiarity she'd heard between them that had been such a difficult pill to swallow. She couldn't help but compare the relaxed tenor of the phone conversation to the tension that still seemed to dominate the room whenever they were together, even now that they were "friends."

Was this what she had to look forward to if she moved back to New Orleans permanently? Sitting around wondering about the women on the other end of his phone line?

The more difficult question: which would she rather wonder about? Whether he was casually dating several women, or in a serious relationship with just one?

Neither.

"You don't get a say," Ivana reminded herself. As Jonathan's "friend" she should root for his happiness, even if he found that happiness with someone else.

She snorted. She strove for kindness in just about everything she did, but her benevolence only went so far.

The messenger app popped up on her computer.

Just heard back from Serena. Want to come into my office?

It had galled her to ask his friend Serena for help yet again, but Ivana couldn't deny that the woman knew her stuff. If circumstances were different, she could imagine herself befriending the immigration attorney.

She approached Jonathan's open office door and knocked twice on the door jamb.

"Come in." He motioned for her to enter.

The moment she sat, his cellphone rang.

"Busy as always," Ivana commented, folding her hands in her lap as she sat.

"This won't take long." He answered the phone in speaker mode. "Hey, did you need something else?"

"Just you," came a female voice. Ivana stiffened. It was the woman he'd been on the phone with earlier. "My meeting was cancelled, so I have an unexpected free hour that I am generously giving to you. Can you meet me here?"

Okay, no. She could not do this. Ivana started to stand.

"Sure," Jonathan answered. "I have few things to discuss with Ivana, but then I'll head right over."

"Ivana? Ivana Culpepper?"

Ivana wasn't sure which rattled her more, the woman's surprised voice or the fact that she knew her name.

"When did you get back in town?" the woman asked.

She frowned, then in a cautious voice, asked, "Indina?"

"Yes, it's me! It's so good to hear your voice," Indina Holmes said. "You should bring her along, Jonathan. She can give us some insight into—"

"Ivana's busy with another project," Jonathan said.

"This won't take long. And I want to pick her brain. Based on what you've told me about your inspiration for this place, I think Ivana should have some input. Don't you?"

A glimpse at Jonathan's embittered expression caused Ivana's curiosity to shoot through the roof. What could this possibly be about?

"We'll be there in a few minutes," he said before disconnecting the call. He looked to her. "You up for a road trip?"

"A road trip?"

"A ten-minute road trip," he said as he gathered a sheaf

of papers from his desk. He slipped them into a tan envelope and closed the metal clasp.

"Sure," Ivana said. "I'll meet you in the lobby."

She returned to the office she'd been provided and uploaded the documents Nicolas had forwarded to the cloud drive. She would review them at home. When she made it to the lobby, she found Jonathan waiting at the edge of LaKeisha's desk. The receptionist, whose frosty feelings toward Ivana had thawed quite a bit in the last week, looked back and forth between the two of them, a curious smile edging up her lips.

"Going out for lunch?" LaKeisha asked.

"I have to meet with Indina Holmes," Jonathan said. "She requested I bring Ivana. This shouldn't take long."

"Your afternoon is clear. You can take all the time you need." She wiggled her fingers, mischief dancing in her eyes. "See you all later."

Ivana caught the agitated look Jonathan lobbed his receptionist's way before gesturing for Ivana to proceed him out the door. She walked down the porch steps and over to the passenger side of his car. She reached for the door handle, only to discover there weren't any.

"Here you go," Jonathan said, reaching around her and pressing an indention she hadn't even noticed. "The door handles retract," he explained.

"Oh," Ivana said. "Does it fly as well?"

He laughed. "Not yet."

She slipped inside the car and ran her hand along the smooth leather seat. Of all the changes he'd made since she left, Ivana was certain the new car was one of necessity. They'd gone car shopping right before the wedding that never took place. He'd wanted style. She'd demanded fuel-efficiency. Based on everything else she'd witnessed since returning home, Ivana was surprised he hadn't bought a gas-guzzling tank of an automobile just to spite her.

"This is a very nice car," she said, once he was seated behind the wheel.

"Thanks." He started the car by pressing a button on the dashboard display screen. He glanced over at her, his smile wry. "I'll save you time from having to Google it. It's one hundred percent electric. I'm reducing my carbon footprint."

A sudden laugh burst from her lips. "You knew I planned to look it up the minute I had the chance, didn't you?"

"I know *you*," he said, amusement shimmering in his eyes.

Ivana held his gaze as they sat in the idling car, a sudden sense of longing overwhelming her. In a soft voice, she said, "I could always count on you to make me laugh."

The instant rush of nostalgia that permeated the air was both powerful and potent. It suffused every inch of the car's interior, thrusting recollections of happier times into the forefront of her mind. Would she ever be able to look at him without recalling those memories they'd shared? Without being pummeled with memories of what she'd had and lost? Did he suffer the same every time he looked at her?

Maybe he was right. Maybe it *was* impossible for them to just be friends.

"We should get going," Jonathan said.

"Yes," she said with a startled jerk. She smoothed her hand along her skirt, but then tucked it against her stomach when she realized her fingers were trembling. "Where exactly are we going?"

"The Warehouse District." He backed out of his

reserved parking space. "I bought a building there. Indina is helping me renovate it."

"Into what?"

"A new club."

Ivana nodded. For the sake of her sanity, she had tried to put her most recent visit to his other nightclub out of her mind, but since they were on the subject...

"It seems as if things are going well at The Hard Court. Sienna said the area's residents really appreciate the parking garage you built."

He shrugged and nodded. "Just trying to be a good steward to the neighborhood."

He took a right onto Julia Street, slowing as he came upon a smoke gray, two-story structure with tall, paned windows. Ivana spotted Indina Holmes standing beneath a small, arched awning that spanned the wide wooden and glass doors. When Jonathan pulled the car to a stop, Indina rushed over, her arms open wide.

"Oh, my goodness! It is *so* good to see you," she said, enveloping Ivana in a monstrous hug the moment she alighted from the car. "You look amazing as always."

"Thank you. It's great to see you too," Ivana said. "And I recently learned congratulations are in order. I met Griffin at Jonah's christening party."

"My new hubby's hot, ain't he?" she said with a grin.

Ivana burst out laughing. "Very hot."

"Let's stop before this one gets jealous," Indina said with a wink, hooking a thumb toward Jonathan.

Ivana began to correct her, but Indina had already moved on to the matter at hand. She patted the black portfolio she held tucked under her arm.

"I printed out a few designs for you to look over. I would have brought my laptop so you could see them in 3D, but it's been acting up lately." She started for the building's entrance. "Now, these are based solely off the specs and pictures you sent me. I may get in there and decide to go an entirely different route. I just never know until I see the space with my own eyes."

She looked over her shoulder at Indina. "I'm happy he brought you along. Figuring out how to recreate this White's place simply from the few pictures I've been able to find online hasn't been easy."

Ivana's steps faltered. "White's?"

"Yes." Indina looked to Jonathan. "You didn't explain the idea to her? He's basing this newest place on some kind of gentlemen's club you used to read about in novels?"

Ivana's breath caught in her throat.

She remembered the day he'd surprised her at her incense stand in the French Market, walking up behind her and snatching the paperback novel she'd been reading from her hands. Even now, she could feel the heat that flushed her face as she awaited his ridicule. It's how her ex-husband, Michael, had always reacted whenever he caught her reading her beloved historical romances.

But Jonathan never mocked her. On occasion, he would even surprise her by having books from her favorite authors hand-delivered to her on their release day.

Ivana was unable to keep the astonishment from her voice. "You're opening a White's?"

She caught the hint of reluctance in his brief nod, as if he were ashamed to admit it.

"Yeah," he answered. "Well, Indina's interpretation of it."

A rush of tenderness engulfed her. In a time when it appeared that he'd tried to erase everything in his life that reminded him of her, it was a challenge to wrap her head around just how much it meant to have him remember this one thing she'd held so dear. Not only remember it, but embrace it.

"Why don't we go inside and look around," Jonathan said as he pulled a key from his pocket and unlocked the door. "Maybe you can share with Indina exactly what it is you envisioned with that place you used to talk about opening."

Still grappling with the significance of the inspiration behind Jonathan's club, she followed Indina around the spacious warehouse, envisioning the scenes from some of her favorite novels playing out in this space.

They stopped in the very center of the building. Sunlight streamed through the tall windows, projecting illuminated rectangles onto the dusty hardwood floors.

"Was this a textile mill at one time?" Ivana asked.

"I think it was, decades ago," Jonathan said.

"I can smell it in the walls," she said, soaking in the structure's history.

"So, what can you tell me about this White's place?" Indina asked.

"It's from the romance novels I read," Ivana said, shaking her head at her obsession with the Regency period, despite the fact that it went against everything she stood for.

"White's is a very exclusive club in London that has been around since the seventeenth century. The gentlemen of the ton—the upper crust of British society—would gather there for conversation, cards, drinks, and other gentlemanly pursuits." She looked over at Jonathan. "Several years ago, Jonathan took me on a trip to London and I was able to see White's in person, but only from the outside. You have to be a member to go inside, and because it remains a men's only club, I will never be able to enter."

"That same day she vowed to open a club like White's, one where everyone would be allowed to come in and enjoy it," Jonathan said.

She looked to him with an impish grin on her lips. "It was my own little defiant fantasy."

His smile was slow and secretive, and she wondered if he was recalling the magical time they'd had together while on that trip.

"I'm liking the sound of this," Indina said. "The thought of a men's only club in this day and age is ridiculous." She clapped her hands together. "So, when it comes to the ambience, we're going for a London gaming club?"

"Yes." Jonathan nodded, his voice once again all business. "Think drinks and quiet conversation after work with a little jazz playing softly in the background. In the evenings, patrons can snack on light fare from the kitchen, but no huge meals. I don't want a full restaurant. I also want a cigar lounge. Cigars are making a huge comeback, among both men and women."

"This is going to be very different from The Hard Court," Indina said.

"It's meant to be," Jonathan said. "In size, scope, and clientele. The people I envision patronizing Campbell's wouldn't step foot in The Hard Court."

"Is that the name you've decided on?" Ivana asked.

He shrugged. "I don't know if White's is named after an actual person, but Campbell's just feels right to me."

"I think it's perfect."

He smiled that smile again, the one that warmed her all the way to her core.

"I'm going to take a few pictures, and then I need to get back to the office," Indina said. She gave Ivana another hug.

"It was so great to see you again. How long are you in town?"

"I..." Ivana hesitated. "For another month or so, I guess."

"That long! Awesome! Then I know I'll see you around. I'm sure Toby and Sienna will have another party soon. Or someone in my family. You know us Holmeses love to get together."

"I've always loved that about your family," Ivana said. "I've missed it. I've missed all of you."

"I know I speak for everyone when I say we are happy to have you back for however long we get to have you," Indina said before departing for the other side of the warehouse.

Ivana turned to Jonathan and was struck by the intensity in his gaze. When he spoke, his voice held a collection of emotions: curiosity, impatience.

Hope.

His eyes boring into hers, he asked, "If you've missed us so much, why go back?"

"FORGET I ASKED THAT."

Jonathan took off for the other side of the building where Indina was busy capturing images of the floors, exposed brick walls, and thick, two-story concrete columns with her phone.

What in the hell was wrong with him? Why'd he even think it was okay to ask Ivana that question?

There was just something about watching her as she ambled around the empty warehouse, recounting that enchanting week they'd spent together in London. It had knocked him off his game. Listening to her talk about their visit to White's evoked memories he'd worked too damn hard to keep buried.

It usually hurt too much to remember, but today it felt different. Today those memories didn't have the same sting.

"I think I have everything I need for now," Indina said. "I'll come up with a few computer animations and bring them to your office later this week."

"That sounds good," Jonathan said. He nodded toward the entrance. "We'll follow you out."

"Wait." Ivana grabbed his jacket sleeve. "Can we stay for a bit longer?"

"Stay," Indina said. "I can see myself out."

Ivana continued to grip his jacket as they waited for Indina to leave. Only after they were alone in the cavernous warehouse did she finally let go, taking a couple of steps to the right to create space between them.

"It's such a beautiful structure," she said. "Would you mind giving me a tour?"

He should have come up with an excuse as to why he absolutely could *not* remain in this building with her. The temptation to forget all the reasons why he shouldn't want her grew with every minute they were together.

Yet, despite the agony being in her presence wrought, lately Jonathan found himself not wanting to be anywhere else. It was masochistic in a way, the pain and pleasure he derived just being near her. Ivana Culpepper had always been more addicting to him than any drug.

As far as he was concerned, this new "let's just be friends" thing they'd been trying for the past two days was a farce. When it came to Ivana, he wanted her to be his everything or nothing at all.

"I understand if you need to get back to the office," she

said. "I was just hoping that you could show me around since we're here."

"No, it's fine," Jonathan said. "You heard what LaKeisha said before we left. My afternoon is completely free."

He stuffed both hands into his pockets to resist the urge to capture hers. The gesture beckoned too many memories of their evening strolls along the Mississippi River levee, or around the duck pond in Louis Armstrong Park.

"Did my fascination with White's really influence your decision to open this new club?" Ivana asked as they began their slow perusal of the warehouse.

"Yes," he admitted. "You're the inspiration behind the entire thing."

She stopped walking. Jonathan looked over to find her staring at him with a look of pure astonishment.

"What?" he asked.

"I still can't believe you would own up to that," she said. "Even if it *is* true."

"Why would you think it isn't true?"

She hunched her shoulder. "It just seems as though you hate me too much to ever—"

"Don't. Please, stop saying that," Jonathan pleaded. He pinched the bridge of his nose, striving to tamp down the sheer torment her remark elicited. "I already told you that I don't hate you. I could never hate you, Ivana."

He regarded her with raw honesty. "But I tried."

Hands still shoved in his pockets, he stepped back until he could rest against the distressed brick wall. "I tried my hardest to hate you. I couldn't stand to be around anything that even reminded me of you."

She winced, then crossed her arms over her chest, hugging her upper body.

"Is that why so many of the things I picked out in the law office are gone?" she asked.

Jonathan struggled to swallow. He nodded.

"It became impossible to walk into that place every day when so much of you remained there. Anything you'd touched was a reminder of what you'd done. So, yeah." He ran both hands down the front of his tie, smoothing out the blue silk. "I made it my mission to erase everything about you from my life. I stopped going to our favorite restaurants, stopped seeing our mutual friends. I even stopped looking at the TV shows we used to watch together. I went an entire year without seeing a single *Law & Order* rerun. Do you know how hard that is to do?" he added with a grin, a poor attempt to lessen the tension drumming between them.

"But I don't understand," Ivana said. "If you spent all this time trying to erase me from your life, why did you decide to open a club that would be a constant reminder of...well, of me?"

Jonathan shoved his hands back into his pockets so she couldn't see him clenching and unclenching his fists. He shifted his feet, nervous energy vibrating from his core out to his extremities.

"Because once I came to terms with what happened three years ago, I realized that I could never be happy if I shut you completely out of my life," he finally admitted. He pulled his bottom lip between his teeth, afraid it would tremble if he didn't. "I also realized that I liked the person I became once I found you, Ivana. You made me a better man. And when you left?" He shook his head. "I didn't like what I saw when I looked in the mirror. In fact, I hated what I'd become."

"Goodness, Jonathan." Her voice quivered. Her eyes...

they held such sadness. "I know it will never be enough, but I truly am sorry for what I did to you."

It was the anguish in her voice that did it. It shattered the armor he'd placed around his heart, destroying the last dregs of resentment he'd fought so fiercely to hang on to.

He couldn't do this anymore. He could not stand here and pretend he wasn't falling in love with her again. That he'd ever fallen *out* of love with her.

"Stop apologizing," he said. "It happened. It's done. And I know that you're sorry. You don't have to keep apologizing."

Jonathan knew that wasn't enough. There was one thing she needed above all else, one thing that would assuage the genuine misery he'd observed in her since her return.

She wanted his forgiveness.

He could do it. He could say the words and take away the pain in her eyes. But would he really *mean* it?

No, he wouldn't. He wasn't there yet. If he spoke the words to her, they would be empty.

"I'm not as angry as I once was," he said instead.

Her eyes widened with cautious hope, the luminous brown orbs taking on a doe-like appearance. Jonathan took a step toward her, then another. His eyes roamed her face.

"I wish I could be," he admitted. "I've been trying so damn hard to fight this. But having you here, remembering how things were when we were together..." He shook his head. "It's been so much harder than I ever thought it would be."

"I know," she whispered. "For me too."

He brought his hand up and smoothed it down her thick, naturally curly hair.

"I don't want to fight it anymore, Ivana."

He shoved his fingers into her hair, holding the back of her head steady as his lips closed over hers. Everything he knew and loved came back to him with that first taste. It was a taste he'd come to cherish, to rely on. A taste that had once filled his world with joy.

A taste he thought he'd never get the chance to experience again.

But here they were, succumbing to the unbelievable chemistry that could never be denied.

He opened his mouth over hers and played at the edges of her lips, coaxing them to part even further so he could sink even deeper into her kiss. Strengthening his grasp on her head, Jonathan spun them around and walked them the two steps back that would bring Ivana's back against the wall.

The soft mewl that escaped her lips sent a rush of fire shooting through his veins. He deepened the kiss even more, thrusting his tongue into her mouth and sweeping it along hers. He brought both hands up to her cheeks and cradled her face between his palms, holding her still while he tasted his fill.

How had he gone so long without this? How had he survived without experiencing the incredible sweetness of her lips on his, the feel of her body pressed up against his? With this one amazing kiss, he'd found everything that had been missing in his life.

Jonathan brought his hands down to her waist and cradled it, his hand practically spanning the entirety of her slim waist. He mentally saw his hands moving upward, but knew he couldn't go there. If his palms found their way to her breasts, he wouldn't be responsible for what happened next.

Instead, with reluctance, he pulled away.

He rested his forehead against hers, their shallow breaths mingling as they both tried to recover from the mind-blowing kiss.

"God, I've missed this," Jonathan breathed.

When he lifted his head he almost smiled at Ivana's shell-shocked expression. He understood. That kiss had sent a seismic jolt zipping through his veins, shocking the hell out of him too.

His breaths still labored, Jonathan backed up a couple of steps. She looked as if she needed some space.

Actually, she looked seconds away from bolting.

She was spooked. He saw it in the dazed, panicked look in her eyes.

"We...uh...we should get back to the office," she said, running a shaking hand through her hair.

"Ivana—" He started to reach for her but thought better of it, remembering what happened the last time she'd been this triggered. He didn't want to send her running again.

"Yeah. Okay," Jonathan said. "We should probably get back."

She scuttled around him, making a beeline for the door.

If not for the bluesy notes from Gary Clark Jr's electric guitar coming through the Tesla's sound system, the ride back to the office would have been completed in total silence. The moment he pulled into his parking spot at the law office, Ivana rushed from the car and into the building. She was already in her office by the time he entered the parlor. She remained there for the rest of the day.

Jonathan spent the remainder of *his* afternoon in equal parts reliving that kiss and debating whether or not to go to her. As much as his body clamored for him to be near her again, something even stronger warned him against moving too fast. Not just for Ivana's sake, but for his own.

He needed to take a step back and evaluate the feelings fomenting within him. Were they simply a reaction to old memories being resurrected, or did this go deeper? Was his willingness to overlook her past transgression a gateway to forgetting what she'd done?

No way. Not a chance.

The devastation of her betrayal and its resulting scars would remain with him until he breathed his final breath. He would never be in danger of forgetting.

But should he allow her betrayal to continue to rule his life? It had robbed him of joy for three long years. What did it mean for them—for what could become of them—now that he'd made the decision to no longer harbor all this resentment?

Jonathan leaned his head back against the headrest and stared up at the plaster ceiling, his mind grappling with the implications of that kiss.

And wondering when he could kiss her again.

Chapter Eight

"YOU DON'T *HAVE* to go in today."

Ivana tossed the belted maxi dress she'd planned to wear onto the chair, and plopped down on the mattress, burying her face in her hands.

Yes, she did have to go in. If she didn't show up at Campbell & Holmes, Jonathan would instantly know it was because she was too cowardly to face him after that kiss they'd shared yesterday.

She fell back onto the bed and covered her eyes with her forearm, breathing through the duration of the full-body shudder that surged within her at the mere thought of that kiss. Tasting his lips again, having his tongue brush against her own; it had kindled a yearning that Ivana knew would not go away anytime soon.

And she thought the regret she'd endured up until this point was intense? It was *nothing* compared to what she would suffer now that she'd had the chance to savor Jonathan's incredible mouth again. The prospect of facing him today made her want to crawl into bed. Because she knew what his response would be. He would say that they'd gotten caught up in the moment. That yesterday was a mistake. That it could never happen again.

And, once again, she would have to come to terms with what she'd had, and what she'd lost.

That voice in her head pleaded with her not to go into the office, but she'd allowed fear to dictate her actions three years ago and the only thing she'd gain from it was heartache. If only she'd been smart enough to ignore that same voice when it cornered her the week before their aborted wedding, she wouldn't be in the predicament in which she now found herself.

It was funny the way the mind worked. Despite knowing that Jonathan was the polar opposite of her first husband, Ivana had become convinced that if she went through with the wedding, she would lose her identity in the same way she had after marrying Michael. In the weeks before the wedding, she'd found herself waking up in the middle of the night in cold sweats, true terror overwhelming her.

She'd told Jonathan she was possibly coming down with something and had offered to move from their bed to the couch. He wouldn't hear of it. He'd told her if she was sick on their wedding day, he wanted to be sick right there with her. That's how much he'd loved her.

Yet she'd run away from him.

But not this time. She would find her damn backbone and face the consequences of yesterday's kiss.

When she arrived at the office an hour later, she discovered the entire place empty, save for LaKeisha.

"Something came up in arbitration on a case Harrison's been working on. Jonathan went to back him up," LaKeisha informed her. "Nicolas should be in soon."

"Good," Ivana said. "I have a few things I wanted to run past him. I'll be in my office."

She stopped short. It was the first time she'd attached any kind of ownership to the space she'd been assigned while working here. She had to be careful. This was a temporary undertaking; it was foolhardy to ascribe any type of permanence to this job.

See what happens after one simple little kiss?

Okay, so maybe simple wasn't the most accurate description. Once you found yourself flush against a wall with a gorgeous man's tongue down your throat, *simple* could no longer be applied.

"Can you let me know when Nicolas gets in?"

"Will do." Ivana started for her office, but stopped and turned when LaKeisha called after her. "Hey, can I ask you something?"

"Sure."

The receptionist brought her elbows up on her desk and rested her chin against her balled fist. "How are things going between you and Jonathan?"

"Uh, okay, I guess," she answered, her brow furrowing at the abrupt subject change.

"I only ask because he seemed...I don't know...more relaxed when the two of you came back from meeting with Indina yesterday. It was the same this morning. I wondered if you had anything to do with his new attitude?"

Ivana felt her face heat. "I'm not sure how to answer that."

"I'm not trying to get in your business or anything," LaKeisha said. She picked up a pen and tapped it against the edge of the old-fashioned logbook she kept on her desk.

"Okay, so maybe I am," she said. "You know I've been with

him a long time, so I've witnessed the many phases Jonathan has been through." There was a trace of accusation in her voice. "The worst I've ever seen him was in the months after you left."

For the first time all week, Ivana experienced a touch of the hostility she'd been subjected to when she first came to work here.

"I'll be honest, when I found out you were back in town, I wanted to strangle you," the receptionist continued. "Not so much for what happened before—he's finally past that, thank goodness. I was more concerned about you waltzing back into his life and turning it upside down again."

"That was never my intention," Ivana said.

"I don't care what your intentions were. What I *do* know is that you devastated him three years ago. And if it happens again, I will come and find you, and we will fight, Ivana. I'm as serious as a heart attack."

Despite her discomfort, Ivana couldn't help but smile. "He's so lucky to have someone like you looking out for him."

"Damn right he's lucky." LaKeisha tossed the pen on her desk and sat back in her chair, cocking her head to the side. "Did you know that I have a degree in Business?" she asked.

Ivana shook her head.

"I was only supposed to be here for the summer after I finished college, just so I could earn enough money to go to grad school."

"Why did you choose to stay?"

"Well, it definitely wasn't for the ridiculous workload. Believe it or not, it wasn't even for the obscene amount of money I get paid to handle that workload," LaKeisha said. "My main reason for working here all these years is out of extreme loyalty to Jonathan. I love that man like a brother."

She grinned. "If he were standing here I would say I love him like a really, really *older* brother." Her expression became more earnest. "I would do anything for him, Ivana. Just...don't hurt him again. I'm begging you. I never want to see him suffer the way he did the first time you left."

The ache that settled in her throat made it hard to swallow.

"I won't hurt him," Ivana assured her. "I promise."

"Good, because I really like you and I don't want to have to fight you," LaKeisha said with a smile as she picked up the ringing phone. "The law offices of Campbell and Holmes," she answered, shooing Ivana away with a little wave.

Ivana went into her office and closed the door behind her. But instead of diving into the work that waited for her, she found herself pondering what the atmosphere must have been like in this office three years ago.

For those first few months after she arrived in Haiti, she would stay awake at night, wondering what was happening back home. She envisioned Jonathan hating her, and soon had it confirmed by Sienna's monthly reports.

It was a testament to the mercy of the God she'd once again started to believe in that Jonathan's hatred had begun to wane. If that kiss they shared yesterday was anything to go on, his enmity toward her had all but dissipated.

Ivana was still too afraid to attach any significance to it. It was a one-time thing, fueled by memories of that romantic trip to London. It probably meant nothing to him.

Resolving to put the matter of yesterday's kiss out of her head, she opened the web browser and skimmed the dozens of immigration related websites she'd bookmarked. Before she knew it, two hours had flown by and her body was screaming for more coffee.

Just as she pushed back from the desk, there was a knock on her partially-opened office door. She looked up to find Jonathan standing in the doorway wearing a charcoal gray suit that fit his body to perfection.

"Good morning," he greeted. "Do you have a minute?"

Her heart immediately began to pound within her chest.

"Um, sure," she said, pulling the chair back to her desk.

He entered the office, closing the door behind him. Ivana tracked his steps as he walked over to the credenza that stood against the wall, just to the right of her desk. He folded his arms across his chest and nodded toward the computer.

"How's the research going?"

"It's going okay," she answered, relieved that he wanted to talk about work and not about what happened in that warehouse on Julia Street yesterday. "Actually, it's going better than okay." She pointed at the monitor. "I've been able to identify a number of places where the current immigration system falls short. I think Campbell & Holmes can fill in those gaps. I want to talk through a couple of things with Nicolas first, but I think I can soon start working on the logistics. I'll send it for your review before I begin, of course."

"Of course," he said. He shoved one hand into his pocket, the movement pushing his jacket back slightly and revealing his trim torso. That body was the thing dreams were made of.

"Is that all?" Ivana asked.

"No," he said. "I was hoping we could talk about yesterday."

And there it was. The topic she'd been anticipating.

More like dreading.

Before he could speak, she held up her palms, staving off his comments.

"I know what you're going to say," she started. "And I agree. Things got a little carried away yesterday."

He settled back against the credenza, crossing his feet at the ankles and folding his arms across his chest again.

"Is that what you think I was going to say?"

"Yes, and I understand," she said. She hunched her shoulders. "Maybe it was the walk down memory lane that did it. Reminiscing about the trip to London and how much fun we had."

"Those were good memories."

"Yeah, they were," she said with a sad smile. That feeling of longing and regret, of lost opportunities and lost love, threatened to overwhelm her again. She could spend the rest of her life apologizing and it would never be enough. No words could ever sufficiently describe the sheer grief she would always feel over missing out on the chance to spend her life with him.

Yet, she was optimistic. The fact that he was talking to her again offered a modicum of hope that they could eventually find their way to some sort of deeper friendship. The last thing she wanted to do was muddy things up by having him think she wanted that kiss to lead to something more. He'd made his feeling abundantly clear on that front.

"I'm sure we can both agree it's best if we just forget about what happened yesterday," Ivana continued. "This project has been going so well—better than I'd anticipated. I'd hate for things to become awkward."

"Hmm..." He nodded. "And you think that kiss yesterday will make things awkward?" he asked as he pushed away from the credenza and came to stand in front of her desk.

"You don't think so?" Ivana asked.

He stood there, his penetrating stare unnerving her. A second later, he hunched a shoulder.

"Maybe you're right. Maybe we should just forget about it. We got caught up in the moment, right?"

"Right," Ivana said. Relief coursed through her, but it was coupled with something else. Something...sad. A pang of sorrow that Ivana accepted as her penance for the pain she'd cause so many people, especially the man standing before her.

She jumped, startled at the knock on her door. "Come in," Ivana called.

Nicolas poked his head into the office. "LaKeisha said you wanted to see me?" He caught sight of Jonathan and came further inside. "Hey, I need to talk to you. Can I come by your office once I'm done in here?"

"Sure," Jonathan said. He looked back at her. "I'm in the office for the rest of the day, so feel free to send along anything you want me to review."

She nodded. "I will. Thanks."

As she watched him walk out the door, Ivana was almost convinced she could learn to be happy living in New Orleans again, as Jonathan's friend.

Or at least she could try.

ROCKING GENTLY in his desk chair, Jonathan tossed the miniature basketball-shaped stress ball from one palm to the other. A grin drew up the corners of his mouth as he thought about how flustered Ivana seemed a minute ago.

Yesterday's kiss had definitely spooked her.

But he'd decided that wasn't necessarily a bad thing.

Her demeanor this morning was reminiscent of how she'd been in those days when they'd first met, when a simple caress of his fingers along her skin turned her into a discombobulated mess of nerves. She'd later admitted to him she'd reacted that way because he'd made her feel things she hadn't wanted to feel. Made her remember she was a grown woman, with grown woman needs.

He liked the fact that he could still knock her off her game with just a kiss. Not that she hadn't done the same to him. He'd spent all night and much of the morning replaying that kiss in his head.

He'd gone into her office prepared with a proposition, but her insistence on speaking first had given him a necessary pause. He could use a bit more time to think about exactly what he wanted.

His phone chimed with a text from Nicolas, inquiring whether or not he was free to talk. Jonathan shot him a quick reply and, a moment later, Nicolas entered the office. It wasn't until he sat in a seat across from his desk and flattened his palms over his thighs that Jonathan noticed the apprehensive lines pulling down the corners of the kid's mouth. His eyes were red, as if he'd been crying, or hadn't slept in a full twenty-four hours.

Worry instantly gripped Jonathan's chest. "What's going on?" he asked.

"It's my grandmother," Nicolas answered. "She's taken a turn for the worse. My mom is down there now, along with two of her sisters. My uncle...he's going. He said he's going."

Nicolas ran both hands down his face. "I need to go too. I want to be there for my mom."

"Go," Jonathan said. "Go and be with your family. Have you spoken to your professors?"

He nodded. "I did that before I came here." He clamped his hands together and dropped his head to his chest.

"Nicolas?"

He looked up and his eyes brimmed with tears. "What if they won't let my uncle back into the country?"

Jonathan got up from his chair and walked over to him. He clamped a hand on his shoulder, giving it a firm squeeze.

"Don't worry about that right now."

"Don't worry about it? How do you suppose I do that?"

"You have more important things to focus on. Starting right now, your only job is to get to your grandmother's and support your family." Jonathan reached into his pocket and took out his billfold. He retrieved the cash he had—three hundred dollars—and stuffed it in Nicolas's hand. "This is to help with travel expenses. I'll transfer more electronically. I know last minute plane tickets can cost a grip."

"You don't have to do that," Nicolas mumbled. "No. Forget I said that. I won't let pride get in the way of getting me down there to see my grandmother."

"I wouldn't have let your pride stop me from helping," Jonathan said. He gave his shoulder another squeeze. "I don't know what will happen when your uncle tries to reenter the country, but I want *you* to know that I'm going to work my ass off to make sure he eventually gets to stay here, permanently."

Nicolas rose from his seat and held a palm out to Jonathan. "Thanks," he said.

Jonathan accepted his hand. "No problem. Now get to packing. Your family needs you."

Once Nicolas left, Jonathan returned to his desk, but nervous energy and an unsettling feeling in his gut had him hopping up from his chair a moment later. He paced the length of his office for a full five minutes before deciding he needed fresh air.

"I'll be out back," he called to LaKeisha as he headed for the rear door. He stepped outside and into the garden his brilliantly talented receptionist had cultivated in the compact courtyard behind the law practice. She'd turned what was once a narrow strip of overgrown weeds and crumbling bricks into a calming—albeit tiny—oasis.

A birdbath that tended to attract several birds throughout the day sat in one corner. Positioned next to it was a stone bench, and next to that, the garden's best feature—a small fountain. The soft gurgle of the water calmed him, especially on days like today, when his mind raced with a billion thoughts.

He sat on the bench and closed his eyes, leaning his head back against the building's exterior.

He heard the door open, but he didn't have to open his eyes to see who'd come out to join him. Her scent—that incredible combination of vanilla, patchouli, and a hint of cinnamon—signaled her approach.

"Hey," Ivana said, her voice tentative. "Mind if I join you?"

He moved over to make room for her on the bench.

"I like what you've done with this space," she said.

"The credit goes to LaKeisha."

"Yeah. She said you only come out here when you have to think really hard or when you're upset about something. Which is it?"

"The latter," Jonathan said. "It's Nicolas."

"What about him? Is he okay?" The urgency in her voice underscored her concern. One wouldn't think she'd only known the kid for such a short time.

"It's his grandmother." Jonathan relayed the information Nicolas had shared regarding his grandmother's health. "He and his Uncle Javier are going to go down there to join the rest of the family."

"Will he...will Nicolas be allowed back in the country?"

"Nicolas is a citizen," Jonathan said. "He has nothing to worry about, but he would be devastated if his uncle wasn't able to come back. His uncle helped to raise him after his father died from cancer." He ran a hand down his face. "I just wish there was more I could do. I feel so damn helpless. How can someone with a law degree who has been practicing for as long as I have not know what to do?"

"Because you're not Superman," Ivana said. "You know your area of the law, but you can't know everything." She captured his chin, turning his head slightly to face her. "And as much as you may want to, you can't help every single person, honey."

Jonathan sat up straight at the endearment.

Her eyes grew wide with dismay. "I'm sorry."

"No. Don't apologize," he said. Jonathan reached a hand out, trailing his fingers along her soft cheek. "I miss hearing you call me honey. I miss so damn much about you, Ivana."

He didn't hesitate this time. This time, when he leaned forward and captured her lips in a soft, slow kiss, he did it with purpose. Need burned within him as he swept his tongue along the seam of her lips, seeking entry. She welcomed him into her mouth, opening for him, her tongue reaching for his.

Jonathan groaned, bringing his hand behind her head and holding her steady, meeting her stroke for stroke. His hunger surged to meteoric heights as he indulged in the richness of her amazing flavor. He could kiss her like this for hours. He *had* kissed her like this for hours. Kissing her—

deriving pleasure from that sensual, addicting mouth of hers —had been life's greatest joy.

He thought he would never have the chance to taste her again. He'd yearned for this for so long. It had haunted his dreams; thinking about those days when they would just lay in bed, sharing a pillow, smiling at each other for hours, kissing each other until they were both breathless. God, how he missed those days.

He brought his other hand to her breast, but she pulled away, pressing a palm against his sternum.

"Not here," Ivana said, the words coming out hoarse.

Jonathan pulled his hand from the back of her head, huffing out a shaky, breathless laugh.

"I should be the one saying that. I just approved the new rules on employee conduct. I guess I should add no kissing in the courtyard to the list." He rested his forehead against hers.

"I don't want to want you," Jonathan whispered. He drew back slightly so he could look into her eyes. "But I've wanted you from the very first moment I saw you."

"You sure about that?" she asked with a shaky laugh. "The first moment you saw me I was railing against you for renovating this building."

"I remember. You were magnificent. So passionate. So damn beautiful." He palmed her cheek. "I remember the feeling that came over me. It was as if something had struck me square in the chest. You've always had this impact, Ivana. Even after you left, there has always been something about you that I just cannot shake. I don't *want* to shake it."

Jonathan thought about the proposition he'd been prepared to make to her this morning. Could he handle this? Was he ready? It was akin to handing over a weapon she could plunge straight into his heart.

But this time it would be different. He couldn't be blindsided if he already knew she would return to Haiti in a few weeks. This time he could guard his heart against the pain and shock of her leaving.

He took her hand in his.

"I'm going to propose something to you. All I ask is that you hear me out," he said.

"Okay," she said, a hint of trepidation in her voice.

"I know too much time has passed for us to ever fully recapture what we once had, but I can't keep pretending that I don't feel something for you, Ivana. And I know you feel something for me too. You can't deny it after that kiss we shared."

Jonathan knew he wasn't playing fair bringing up the kiss. But what had playing fair ever gotten him? He was done playing fair. He was ready to go after what he wanted. And, right now, he wanted *her*.

"Be with me," he said. "While you're here, I want you to be with me."

She went completely still. "Jonathan—"

"I'm not saying we take up where we left off. That can't happen." He wouldn't allow it. "But I want to be with you."

A shadow of uncertainty flashed across her features as she continued to stare at him with that wary look in her eyes.

"Are you sure about this?" she asked.

"No," he answered truthfully. "A part of me wants to take back everything I just said." He shook his head. "Admitting how I really feel gives you too much damn power over me, but what else can I do, Ivana?"

He captured her hand and placed it over his heart. "I'm scared to trust you with this, but it's yours. It's been yours since the minute we met." He caressed her jaw. "You are the love of my life, Ivana Culpepper. Whether I like it or not. I don't want to spend any more time mourning what we lost. I want to enjoy this time we have together *now*, and not just as your friend."

Palming her cheek, Jonathan closed in on her, capturing her mouth in a slow, mind-drugging kiss. He teased the edges of her lips, skating his tongue along the closed seam, gently probing until she finally relented. When she relaxed her lips and let him inside, he found heaven.

The groan that escaped his throat was one of both pleasure and torment. It frightened him, just how easily he could lose his mind over her. With just these few kisses he was halfway there.

He tilted her head to the side and deepened the kiss, plunging his tongue into her mouth and sweeping inside, dipping into every warm crevice. Her taste was so intoxicating, so familiar. And so damn worthy of his time and attention.

He needed this. Needed *her*.

This might turn out to be the biggest mistake of his life. But to be with her like this again, he was willing to risk it.

Chapter Nine

"HIGHER! HIGHER!"

"Are you sure?" Ivana called as she added a touch more emphasis to her push on the little girl's back.

"Yes! Higher!" Elsie yelled.

She'd been in the middle of cleaning her mother's kitchen cabinets—busy work on her part, because the cabinets had been as spotless as everything else in Sylvia's house —when Lilo called. One of her standing clients needed an emergency photo shoot, and Lilo's usual babysitter was out of town. Ivana had jumped at the chance to babysit Elsie, and not only as a means to assuage the guilt she still felt over the way she'd left things with Lilo three years ago. Getting to know her friend's daughter was important to her.

The fact that her friend even *had* a daughter was still mind-blowing. In all the years they'd shared a house, Lilo had never mentioned wanting kids. A much sought-after photographer, she'd spent much of her time traveling from one photo shoot to the next.

But apparently she'd also wanted to be a mother. And she'd made that dream happen.

Ivana tried to ignore the hurt that pierced her chest. It wasn't easy. When she envisioned her life at this age, it had included kids. Up until three years ago, it had included her and Jonathan's children. Of all the things she'd lost when she decided to do her disappearing act, missing out on the chance to bring Jonathan's child into this world hurt her the most.

She never thought three short years would make much of a difference. But when those three short years came at such a critical time in a woman's life, they could mean everything. There were more and more women getting pregnant well into their forties, but Ivana wasn't sure she would be one of them. She'd missed her opportunity.

Of course, she could always adopt, just as Lilo had. She'd lost count of the number of children who'd been orphaned in the few years she'd been in Haiti. It would be a blessing to raise just one of them.

But she didn't want to do it alone. If she ever got the chance to raise a child, she would want to do so with Jonathan at her side.

As if she'd conjured him simply by thinking about him, her cell rang and his name lit up the screen. Ivana fitted the phone between her shoulder and ear while she continued to push Elsie on the swing.

"Hey there," she answered.

"Hey there yourself," he replied. His rich voice triggered goosebumps that instantly formed on her skin.

"Are you doing any better?" she asked. "Or have you been spending more time in the garden?"

"No garden time for me today. I was hoping I'd have some *Ivana* time."

Heat shot down her spine, her pulse quickening as she permitted herself a millisecond to indulge in a fantasy she had no business thinking about in the middle of the day. She knew this was risky, allowing herself to feel these feelings again. But how could she say no? Being the object of Jonathan Campbell's affection again was like a drug, heady and exciting and just a little bit dangerous.

"So, do you have time for me?" he asked.

She gave Elsie another push. "What about Ivana time, plus one little girl?"

"Higher!" Elsie yelled.

He paused. Then, "Where are you?"

"Cabrini Playground. I'm on babysitting duty."

"Are you babysitting for Sienna?"

"I said *one* little girl, not a couple of adorable demons and a colicky baby." She laughed. "I'm watching Lilo's daughter while she's out on a photo shoot."

"Lilo's daughter? What did I miss?"

His incredulity was yet another indication he'd cut himself off from everything that reminded him of her. Although, Sienna didn't know about Lilo's daughter either, so maybe it was her old roommate who'd cut herself off.

"I'll explain once you get here," Ivana said.

She ended the call with Jonathan and pulled back on the swing's coated chains, halting its forward motion.

"What do you say we hit the slides?" Ivana asked.

"Yes!" Elsie jumped off the swing. She turned and planted her hands on her bony hips. "Were you talking to your boyfriend on the phone?"

Ivana felt herself blush. It was downright pitiful that a grown woman would have such a reaction to a little girl's innocent question.

"He's a really good friend," she answered.

Elsie gave her a look that was wise beyond her years.

What kind of stuff had Lilo allowed this little one to watch on television? It had been nearly forty years since she was Elsie's age, but Ivana was sure she'd had no concept of boyfriend and girlfriend back then.

They had only been at the slide/jungle gym/rock climbing contraption for ten minutes when a sleek, black Tesla parallel parked in one of the spots on Dauphine Street. Ivana couldn't quell the frantic beating of her heart even if she tried.

She didn't try. She loved this feeling. Craved it. Just being near him brought about the most exhilarating rush she'd felt in ages.

Jonathan walked up to them dressed in basketball pants and a long-sleeved Philadelphia 76ers T-shirt. The sight of him in a tailored suit made her mouth water, but this? This made her knees buckle and caused her nipples to grow tight.

She knew the kind of mood he was in right now: chilled and relaxed. How many Saturdays had she spent with him dressed like this, cradled against him as they lay together on his couch? He would slip a hand inside her shirt and caress her breasts until she stripped out of her clothes and straddled him.

A delicious shudder pulsed through her.

"Hello," Jonathan greeted, planting a chaste kiss on her cheek. His smile had her wondering if he could tell what she'd been thinking, but then he turned his attention to Elsie.

"Who do we have here?"

Elsie proudly provided her name, then immediately remarked on Jonathan's height. Before he could reply, she began to prattle on about the book her mother was currently reading to her about a little boy who wouldn't stop growing.

Ivana couldn't get a word in edgewise as Jonathan stood there conversing with the five-year-old as if they were old friends.

Elsie placed her hand in his and guided him to the jungle gym. He picked her up, placed her on the colorful playground equipment's highest peak, then instructed her to fall into his arms. Elsie stretched her arms out as he hoisted her into the air, flying her around as if she were an airplane.

A wave of bittersweet longing overwhelmed Ivana as she observed the two of them. He would have made such an amazing father.

Her eyes never leaving them, Ivana backed up until she reached the swings. She settled into one and slowly rocked back and forth, laughing when Elsie yelled at Jonathan to lift her higher. Lilo had better watch it. She had a potential high-wire walker on her hands.

"Don't tell me you had to call for backup?"

Ivana twisted on the swing, turning to find her old roommate walking toward her.

"No, I did not," she answered with a laugh. "Backup arrived of his own accord."

Lilo took the swing to her right. She gestured toward Jonathan and Elsie.

"So, how is that going?" she asked.

"Can't you tell? Elsie had him wrapped around her little finger within two seconds of meeting her."

"You know that's not what I'm talking about," Lilo said.

Yes, she did know. But she was unsure how to answer the question.

"It's hard to say," she answered honestly. "We aren't the same people we were three years ago—we'll never be those people—so it's not as if things can ever be the same."

It was hard not to squirm under Lilo's scrutiny. After a few uncomfortable moments, her friend said, "You still love him."

It was a statement, not a question.

Once again, Ivana decided to go with honesty. "I never stopped."

She met Lilo's sad smile with one of her own. But then her friend's face brightened.

"Hey there, handsome," Lilo said, rising from the swing to meet Jonathan, who carried Elsie on his shoulders. "It's been too long."

"I'd say so," Jonathan said. "I didn't know anything about my new girlfriend here."

"I'm not your girlfriend. You're too old," Elsie said.

Ivana laughed so hard she nearly fell off the swing. She rose and walked over to where the others stood. "I agree, he is a bit old," she said.

"Hey!" Jonathan's affronted expression sent them all into a fit of laughter.

"How about you call him Uncle Jonathan," Lilo said. She turned to Ivana. "Thanks for coming through for me. Based on my best estimation, I should be able to call on you at least another dozen times to make up for lost babysitting duty."

"I'm not keeping count," Ivana said, smoothing a hand down the five-year-old's braided hair. She place a kiss on Elsie's cheek, then did the same to Lilo's before mother and daughter took off for Lilo's Volkswagen Bug.

"That is one adorable little girl," Ivana said as she watched them walk away.

"One would never know she was adopted," Jonathan said from just behind her. She could feel his breath on her neck. "She's the spitting image of Lilo, both in looks and personality."

"Lord help the world." Ivana laughed.

Jonathan captured her shoulders and tugged her a couple of steps back, guiding her to the swing she'd vacated moments ago. He pulled back slightly on the chains. "You game?"

She looked at him over her shoulder, delighting in the mischievous glint in his eyes. She nodded and braced herself.

He hauled the corded chain back even more and then gave her backside a firm push. Ivana went soaring in the air, the wind whipping across her face as she swung like a pendulum. He put a bit more into every push, sending the swing at least six feet into the air. She kicked her legs, relishing the carefree feeling. In this moment, for the first time in so very long, she felt pure, unadulterated joy. It was as if all the anxiety and pain of the past few years had melted away. God, how she missed this feeling.

"Don't!" she squealed when Jonathan started to push her even higher.

"Be a daredevil."

"What if I slip off?" she called over her shoulder.

He halted her mid-swing, catching her by the waist and wrapping an arm around her middle. "I'm here to catch you," he whispered against her ear.

That shudder ran through her again, hotter and more intense than before.

He released her far too soon, launching her forward with a giant push. Ivana let out a gleeful peal as she tipped her head back and smiled at his upside down form.

"Okay, that's enough swinging," she said, allowing the swing's momentum to slow to a stop.

Jonathan rounded the front of the swing and grabbed onto the coated chains. He leaned forward, encasing her in a cocoon made of his broad shoulders and chest. A sweet, gentle gleam shone in his eyes.

"You're beautiful when you let go like this," he said.

His words triggered an unexpected rush of heat. He would tell her the same thing when she let herself go during another activity they used to engage in. Ivana squeezed her thighs together, remembering the pleasure she would experience when she handed herself over to him completely and left him in charge of her pleasure.

"I missed hearing your laugh," Jonathan said.

"And I missed hearing yours," she said. "It was a joy to watch you laughing with Elsie. You would make a wonderful father, Jonathan."

He ran his hand along her jaw. "Do you have any idea how much I wanted to have a baby with you?"

Ivana shut her eyes and felt a tear roll down her face. The pad of his thumb brushed across her cheek, wiping it away.

"Don't," he said.

She opened her eyes and tried her hardest to smile, but she was unable to staunch the bittersweet regret that threatened to overwhelm her. They stared at each other for several long, quiet moments. No words needed to be said. They both knew exactly what the other was thinking, what they were remembering, what they were regretting.

Time lost. Missed opportunities. What could have been.

"We're not supposed to talk about this stuff, remember?" Jonathan said. "If we only have this short time together, I want to spend it creating new memories with you, not thinking about the past. Is that still okay for you?"

She nodded.

"Good," he said. He pressed his lips against the crest of her cheekbone, kissing away the tear that escaped. He brought his mouth to hers.

"Because I'd rather do this than talk," he said before connecting his lips to hers.

HORRIFIED, Ivana covered her mouth with her hand as she read through another firsthand account of day-to-day life provided by people from Nicolas's community. All were anonymous and all were devastatingly heartbreaking. She couldn't imagine having to live in constant fear of being ripped away from her loved ones.

She struggled to swallow past the lump of emotion in her throat while reading the story of a young mother who was afraid to bring her sick daughter to the hospital after rumors of ICE raids began to circulate around the neighborhood. To her astonishment, a number of the atrocities detailed in the letters occurred years ago, well before she left for Haiti. Ivana had prided herself on helping this city's most vulnerable residents. To know that she'd been here and had no idea this was going on ate at her conscience.

"I don't know what you're reading, but it must be pretty intense."

Ivana brought a startled hand to her chest at the interruption. She'd become so engrossed in the testimonial that she wasn't aware LaKeisha had even entered the office until the receptionist was standing in front of her desk.

"Sorry. Didn't mean to scare you," LaKeisha said. "Just came in to ask a favor. I'm heading to City Hall to look up a few things for Harrison's case. I won't be gone long, but I'm expecting a package to come by courier. If it arrives while I'm away, can you please sign for it? Jonathan needs the documents this afternoon."

"Sure, no problem," Ivana said. She returned her attention to the sheaf of loose-leaf papers in her hands, but after a few moments, looked up to find LaKeisha still standing there, a soft smile crinkling her eyes at the corners.

"Is there something else?" Ivana asked.

She shook her head, but then said, "Actually, yes, there is. Thank you."

She tilted her head to the side. "For what?"

"Making my boss happy again," LaKeisha said. "Personally, I thought he was a fool for hiring you to work on this project, but he's a pleasant fool when you're around, and for that, I'm thankful. Just remember what I said. It's been a while since I've been in a fight. I'm primed and ready."

"Put your boxing gloves away," Ivana said, her lips quirking up with her smile. "I already told you I won't give you a reason to fight me."

"Damn," LaKeisha said, snapping her fingers.

She laughed, but once she was alone again, Ivana put her elbows on the desk and covered her face in her palms.

What was she was doing here? Other than trying to have her cake and eat it too?

If she were as decent a human being as she professed to be, she would have turned Jonathan down when he approached her with his proposition. Because even though the very foundation of this thing they had going was predicated on the assumption that she would be returning to Haiti soon—that he wouldn't be caught off guard the way he'd been three years ago—she couldn't guarantee that Jonathan wouldn't be hurt again.

Maybe he was right. Maybe, this time, it would be

different. It wasn't up to her whether or not he would be hurt in the end. He had just as much control over the outcome as she did.

They'd both entered into this with eyes wide open, agreeing to push all their previous baggage to the side and just enjoy each other's company for the next few weeks. Ivana had to admit that they were off to an enchanting start.

Last night's visit to Cooter Brown's for fries covered in gravy and cheese—her absolute favorite late-night cheat treat—had been their third date this week. They'd started with the movies Monday night, and then dinner at a new Jamaican restaurant on Wednesday. Last night, when they left the bar in the city's Black Pearl neighborhood and stopped for ice cream at Angelo Brocato—another favorite— it had felt like old times.

But it was an illusion. They were only pretending this unencumbered bliss was the real thing because it would make it easier when she returned to Haiti.

But what if she didn't go back?

That was still a question she had yet to answer. She'd received an email from her supervisor at Operation: Heal just this morning, inquiring about her physical and mental health. Patience had ended the email with a reminder that Ivana's three years in Haiti was twice as long as most volunteers put in and that it would be perfectly acceptable if she chose not to return.

If she didn't know better, Ivana would question whether or not Patience liked having her there. But she knew the woman was only looking out for her. As the person who'd found her clutching her chest and doubled over in pain, Patience had borne witness to the toll the grueling relief work had taken on Ivana's body.

She was proud of what she'd accomplished in Haiti, but she knew it was time to move on.

If only she could decide what she wanted to move on *to*.

Maybe you can do this?

No, she couldn't. She absolutely could not work here full-time. Once everything was in place, Jonathan would need to hire someone well-versed in immigration law to head this up. But in the process of what she'd originally considered just a passion project, she'd discovered she had a bit of a knack for organization and project management. Maybe she could find a worthwhile association that would allow her to utilize her skills?

She was doing the right thing by keeping her potential plans to herself. Heck, she wasn't even sure she knew what those plans were just yet. When the time came to make a decision, it was possible she would decide that returning to New Orleans wasn't for her. It wasn't as if she had to come back to her hometown if she lived stateside again. As long as she was close enough so that she could visit and not miss out on any more important family milestones, that's what mattered. Why get Jonathan's hopes up if she wasn't going to live here?

Ivana went back to the accounts she'd been reading. She wanted to include short quotes and anecdotes in the final proposal she put together for Jonathan. She'd just set the phone down so that she could run to the break room for a bottle of water when her phone started to buzz with Sienna's ring tone.

"Hey, what's up?" Ivana said, answering the video call. She squinted at the screen. "Why does it look as if you're on an airplane?"

"Because I am on an airplane."

"And you're FaceTiming me? Ugh, Cee Cee, you're one

of those people I hate. Airplanes are for quiet reading time." Ivana sat up straight. "Wait a minute. *Why* are you on an airplane? Where are you going?"

"That's why I'm calling," her sister said, her mouth scrunching up with her grimace. "I know we were supposed to help you move into Granny Elise's house this weekend, but Aria has a concert at the Hollywood Bowl tomorrow night and we decided it would be the perfect opportunity to bring the kids to Disneyland."

Ivana rolled her eyes.

"Please don't be mad," Sienna said. "If you can hold out another week at Mom's, we'll help you move in when I come back."

Yeah, that wasn't happening. She loved her mother because she'd given her life, but if she had to spend another week in that house Ivana was pretty sure she would end up at Tulane and Broad. She didn't come back to this city just to land herself in New Orleans's Central Lockup for choking her own mother.

"I'll figure something out," Ivana said. She was already thinking about how much money she could spare to hire someone to help her move. It's not as if she had a ton of stuff. It was more about getting the house in order after the last tenant vacated it than hauling her meager belongings there.

"I'm sorry, Vonnie."

"Don't worry about it," Ivana said. "Go enjoy Disneyland with the kids. Although, I'm not sure how much you can enjoy it with an infant in tow."

"That infant has a daddy who is perfectly capable of taking care of him why the kids and I ride the Tea Cups and Haunted Mansion," Sienna said. "Uh-oh, I'm getting looks from the flight attendant. Let me log off. Love you, honey."

"Love you," Ivana said before the screen went black. She set the phone on the desk and blew out an agitated breath. "Well, this is just great."

"Do you need a hand this weekend?"

She turned in the chair to find what had become a familiar sight, Jonathan casually taking up space in her doorway. He leaned a shoulder against the doorjamb, one hand in his pocket, the other holding a cup of coffee.

He gestured to her phone with his chin. "It sounds as if Sienna and Toby bailed on you."

"Can't say I blame them." Ivana laughed. "If I had to choose between Disneyland and cleaning a dirty house, I'd choose Mickey Mouse too."

"I can help you," he said, as he made his way over to her desk. "I'm a bit offended you haven't asked me yet."

She hadn't asked because she already felt herself slowly falling for him again. *Slowly?* There was nothing slow about this; she was diving head first into mind-numbing deep love. Not as if she'd ever fallen *out* of love with him.

Ivana felt she was due an award for the amount of restraint she'd exhibited this week. There were so many times she'd wanted more than just the few kisses they'd shared. How much harder would it be to fight those urges if the two of them were alone in that house all day? That was asking for trouble.

But she *did* need help moving in. She could find some measure of control, couldn't she?

"If it wouldn't be too much of a hassle," Ivana said.

"If it would be a hassle, I wouldn't have offered." His teasing smile was nothing short of adorable.

He came around her desk and rested his backside against it. The sight of the slacks stretching across his taut thighs was decidedly more than adorable. It was scrumptious.

"I know how much you must *love* living with your mother," he continued with his teasing, and Ivana burst out laughing. He caressed her jaw. "Let me help you."

"Okay," she said.

"What time should I be there?"

"Whenever you can make it."

"Let's try this again," Jonathan said. "What time do *you* plan to arrive?"

"I'll be there by nine a.m.," she said.

"So will I. I'll bring breakfast." His phone beeped. "That's the reminder I set for a conference call I need to take," he said. "It'll probably go on for a couple of hours, so if I don't see you before you leave for the day, I'll see you tomorrow."

He winked as he pushed away from the desk and left the office.

Ivana shoved the papers to the side and dropped her head on the desk. She knew leaving a second time wouldn't be easy, but now it was clear that leaving with her heart intact would be downright impossible.

JONATHAN PULLED up in front of the wood-framed house in the city's Bywater neighborhood and realized how long it had been since he'd been to this part of the city. Other than the occasional visit to one of his favorite restaurants four streets over, it had been well over a year since he'd driven these particular pothole-ridden streets.

The Bywater was one of New Orleans's quirkier areas; in a city that thrived on quirkiness, that was saying a lot. But there was something cozy about the eccentricities found in the colorful homes. The area fit Ivana to a tee.

He took a moment to relish the pure pleasure that cascaded through him just at the thought of her. It was jarring, how quickly his attitude had changed. Just a few weeks ago the mere mention of her name made his blood boil.

Now? Now, he *craved* her.

Jonathan couldn't remember a time when he'd been so eager to walk through those doors of his law practice as he was these days, knowing she would be there, working so diligently just a couple of offices down from his. She had him practically running red lights to make it to work in the morning.

It was dangerous, the way he found himself yearning just to hear her voice. He knew he was setting himself up for the hardest fall. But he couldn't bring himself to care. Not now. Not when he had her back in his life.

She completed him. His world was a thousand times better when she was a part of it.

An unsettling weight landed in his gut. It would kill him when she left in a few weeks. He was talking total annihilation. Heart ripped in two and flushed down the toilet. But if he thought about that, it would wreck him. He would focus on the here and now, and savor every second he had with her.

Though, when it came to savoring Ivana, something way more enticing than just spending time with her came to mind.

A strangled groan escaped his lips.

If there was one thing that was sure to get him in trouble, it was thinking about *that*. But damn, how could he *not* think about joining his famished body with hers? Those few stolen kisses they'd shared had ignited a fire that, if he were being honest with himself, had never been extinguished, even in the three years since they'd been apart. It had lain dormant for a while, but those embers had always burned for her.

After tasting the delicious flavor of her kiss again, Jonathan wanted more. He wanted to lock her up in his house for an entire week and take them both on the kind of pleasurable journey that would make up for the years they'd been apart.

Stop, he pleaded with his mind. If he didn't put a halt to this kind of thinking he would never be able to step into that house and face Ivana without her knowing exactly what was on his mind.

But would it really come as a surprise to her? She had to know how much he wanted her. It wasn't as if he'd done much to hide his feelings since they visited the warehouse on Julia Street.

Taking a few moments to gain some control over himself, Jonathan sucked in a deep breath and started for the house. He knocked on the door and heard her yell, "Come on in. It's unlocked."

Unlocked? She may have been gone for a while, but it wasn't long enough for her to forget how dangerous this city could be.

"Where are you," he called as he walked inside. "And why are you in here with the door unlocked?"

"In the kitchen," Ivana answered. "And I figured I'd hear anyone who came in."

Jonathan made his way to the rear of the house where the kitchen was located. It was a peculiar setup, but common in many of the shotgun houses native to New Orleans.

He entered the kitchen and stopped dead in his tracks. She was on her hands and knees, scrubbing a spot on the floor. Her narrow hips and pert, round ass looked amazing in the jean cutoffs she wore. He wanted to drop to his knees and plant his face directly in that ass.

He had to swallow another moan as his entire body began to crave her with an intensity Jonathan knew it would take forever to fight.

So why the hell was he fighting it? Why not just come out and tell her that she was on his mind twenty-four seven?

She turned around and smiled. "Hey. Thanks for coming."

She had a smudge of dirt on the tip of her nose and the crest of her right cheekbone. It somehow made her look even more beautiful.

"You didn't get here at nine o'clock," Jonathan pointed out. "There's no way you've only been working for," he looked at his watch, "Fifteen minutes."

"Sylvia's neighbor woke up the entire neighborhood by cutting his lawn at seven a.m."

"On a Saturday?"

"On a damn Saturday," she said. "Once I realized there was no going back to sleep, I decided to get a head start on cleaning up this place. And it's a good thing I did." She stood and plopped her hands on her hips. "Just look at this place! How do you accumulate this amount of grime in just six months? I swear, whoever Sienna rented this place to didn't pass a mop on these floors a single time. It's disgusting."

"We've got all day to clean up. Have some breakfast first," he said, holding up the coffee tray he'd brought with him. He'd wedged the white paper bag with the cinnamon rolls between the two cups.

"I need that," she said, reaching for a coffee.

I need you.

The truth of those three little words seared him like a hot, metal brand, imprinting on his chest, on his very heart. He needed her. Always. No matter what happened between them, his life would never be complete without her in it.

It was a sobering thought to know that another human being could hold such power over him. What scared him the most was that he couldn't do a damn thing about it. He'd tried not to want her, but he could no more deny his need for her than he could deny his own name. The best Jonathan could do was learn to manage the emotions she evoked simply by her nearness.

She took a sip of her coffee, which resembled weak tea more than coffee because of the amount of cream she preferred, and released a satisfied sigh.

"Goodness, but that hits the spot." Ivana motioned to the bag. "I smell cinnamon."

"Cinnamon rolls from Revelation. Wash up and I'll set these out for us. I think we can get more done once we've fueled up."

While she washed the grime from her hands, Jonathan ripped the paper bag down the center and used it as a placemat, setting two thick, gooey cinnamon rolls out for both of them. Ivana took a seat at the table and brought one foot up onto the wooden chair. She created such a devastatingly beautiful picture, even in cutoff jeans and a plain yellow tank top. It was that willowy frame and soft brown skin that he couldn't get enough of.

He'd noticed the faint lines that creased her eyes weeks ago. They hadn't been there before she left. They didn't take away anything, only added to her overall grace and allure.

He couldn't help but wonder about the source of those lines. Was it just aging? Was it a result of the hard living conditions she'd endured in Haiti? Stress from the poverty she'd witnessed?

Would those lines—as beautiful as they were—have ever appeared if she hadn't left him?

He still wanted to know why. Why had she stolen those three years from him? When he thought of the time they'd missed out on, how much they could have loved and shared over these past few years, Jonathan wanted to rage.

But where would raging get him? Making her feel horrible for what she'd done three years ago would only serve to ruin their day. It would put a damper on the little time they had left together before she once again went off to save the world. There were so many more enjoyable things he would rather they do with that time.

As they nibbled on their breakfast, they talked about the program she was putting together for him. She warned that she would soon reach the point where she no longer had the expertise to go further.

"Maybe it's time you consider posting about the job on some hiring sites," she said.

"You're probably right," he said.

Jonathan had all intentions of hiring Nicolas to run the program, but things were still so up in the air with his young mentee. With everything going on in his life, he wasn't sure if Nicolas was prepared to tackle something of this magnitude. Maybe he could contact Serena, ask her if she knew of anyone well-versed in immigration law who was on the hunt for a job.

He wouldn't bring that up right now. He didn't want to

mention Serena after what happened the last time he'd called his ex bed-partner while in Ivana's presence.

Jonathan heard the rumbling of a truck coming down the street a few moments before a horn beeped.

"That's probably my furniture," Ivana said.

"You bought furniture?" Jonathan asked. For someone who wouldn't be in town long, it struck him as strange that she'd invest in furniture.

"Just enough to make the house livable," she said.

The delivery men unloaded four huge cardboard boxes, along with a mattress and box spring. Once they were alone again, Jonathan used Ivana's house key to slice through the packing tape.

"Why don't we do this in the living room?" Ivana suggested. "I've cleaned the floor in there."

They pushed the boxes into the living room and began unpacking the contents. As they put together the coffee table, Jonathan couldn't help but tease her.

"Do you remember the last time you tried to put together a piece of furniture?" he asked.

She rolled her eyes. "You're going to bring up that bookcase, aren't you?"

His head flew back with his laugh. She'd bought a bookcase when she'd moved into his condo years ago, and had insisted on putting it together herself. She'd been so proud of her accomplishment...until the top shelf collapsed under the weight of three measly paperback novels.

"Laugh all you want," she said, her nose tipped up in the air. "I'll have you know that I helped to build over a dozen homes with Operation: Hope. My skills with a screwdriver have greatly improved, thank you very much."

"Have they?" He leaned closer and, knowing the reaction his words would yield, whispered against her ear,

"Maybe I can get a little demonstration of those skills later on."

Her light brown cheeks turned beet red.

Jonathan knew damn well that nothing but trouble could come from this flirting, but he didn't care. Making Ivana blush was his favorite pastime.

No. That was a lie. Making her *scream* was his favorite pastime.

He wanted to hear that throaty, pleasure-soaked scream so damn bad. The sound haunted him at night. It was etched into his brain, a ghost from his past that his mind refused to rid itself of.

Pushing memories of her clinging to him as she screamed in ecstasy from his brain, he pointed to the plain white coffee table.

"I have to admit, this table is nothing like you. I think a trip to that unclaimed furniture place in St. Roch is in order."

"Oh, you do know how to tempt me, don't you?" she said, a mischievous grin tilting up her lips.

Jonathan studied her for a moment before brushing a smudge of dirt from her cheek and murmuring, "I made a sport out of tempting you. Or have you forgotten?"

Her amused expression morphed into something... different, something intense. Her gaze dropped to his lips. "There are some things a girl just can't forget, no matter how much she tries."

"Did you try to forget me?" Jonathan asked, the words coming out gravely. Husky.

She brought her eyes back to his and slowly shook her head. "No," she whispered. "It was the opposite." Her eyes roamed his face. "I clung to thoughts of you. For a long time those thoughts of you were the only thing that got me through the night."

Her delicately spoken words lit a fire inside him that Jonathan didn't even attempt to douse. He closed the short distance between them, connecting his mouth with hers.

She hesitated for a moment, but after a gentle urging of his tongue against her lips, she relented, opening her mouth and welcoming him in. He quickly deepened the kiss, sweeping his tongue inside and tangling with hers. It was erotic as hell, and enough to set his skin ablaze.

A low moan climbed up his throat as he feasted on her intoxicating flavor. He could never figure out exactly how to describe it. Something spicy and sweet and purely Ivana; that's what this taste was. It was the most delicious essence in the universe and he would never get tired of consuming it.

He lifted her into his arms, wrapping her long legs around his waist. Then, with only one thing on his mind, Jonathan carried her to the bedroom and placed her on the new mattress. He joined her, slipping his hand underneath her tank top and pulling down the bra cup that covered her right breast.

When it came to breasts he'd always preferred those that were so big they nearly smothered him. Until he met Ivana. Her small, round breasts were perfect for him. He closed his palm over her and made slow circles around her pert nipple, his skin tingling as it slowly beaded as a result of the attention he paid to it.

"God, I've missed this, Ivana." He dipped his head and sucked on her nipple through the tank top. This damn fabric was in his way. He wanted to taste her. He needed to feel that tight nub against his tongue more than he needed his next breath.

Lifting her shirt off, Jonathan pushed her bra up her chest, exposing both breasts to his eyes, teeth and tongue. He lavished the tender mounds with long, slow licks, flicking his tongue across first one nipple and then the next. As he closed his mouth over her right breast, sucking nearly the entire thing into his mouth, his hand slid between them and, with deft fingers, he flicked the snap on her jean shorts. As soon as he had access, Jonathan slipped his hand inside, past the rim of her satin panties and into the nest of damp curls.

His body grew hard at the sensation of the wet folds of her sex sliding between his fingers. He parted the swollen flesh and found the bundle of nerves at her cleft with his thumb. As he pressed against it, he dipped one finger inside.

A mewl escaped her throat, sending a shock of sensation along his spine.

"Do you have a condom?" she asked in a raspy voice.

"Mmm hmm," he murmured against her breast. He removed his hand long enough to grab the wallet from his back pocket. As he retrieved the condom, Ivana pulled her bra over her head and shucked the jean shorts and panties from her hips. She kicked them onto the floor, then reached for his shirt. Jonathan sent it the way of her shorts, then did the same with the basketball shorts he'd thrown on this morning.

In a matter of minutes they'd gone from putting together furniture to lying atop her new, bare mattress, buck naked in the middle of the morning. Jonathan didn't think life could get any more perfect.

That is, until Ivana reached down and closed her soft hands around his throbbing dick. He pitched his head back as she squeezed him, moving her closed fist up and down his hardening flesh. She took the condom from him and opened it. Jonathan watched as she rolled the latex over his erection. When she laid back on the mattress and let her legs fall open, he found heaven.

Three years.

He'd been waiting three years for this. He'd all but convinced himself that he would never experience loving her like this again. He thought the image of her beautiful, naked body was something he could only conjure up in a dream.

But this wasn't some mirage. She was here. And she was his.

Even if it was only for a little while.

Fitting his hands on the underside of her thighs, Jonathan lifted her knees and pushed them back toward her head. Looking into her eyes, he found the entrance to her body and plunged in with one smooth, deep stroke. Her head pitched back as another moan climbed out of her throat.

Pleasure coursed through him. His body gloried in the delicious sensation of finally being joined with her again.

"Dammit, Ivana," Jonathan gritted through his teeth. "Why'd you make me wait so long to feel this again?"

"I'm sorry," she said with a whimper. "Please...please." She thrust her hips upward and Jonathan met them with another deep plunge. Bracing his hands on either side of her, he dipped his head and sucked on her nipple while his hips pistoned up and down. She met him stroke for stroke, lifting her hips and bowing her back, forcing him to take her breast into his mouth.

Jonathan captured her waist and flipped them over on the bed so that she straddled him. Her wild hair looked like a crown, the crinkly curls falling around her shoulders in riotous waves.

"I've missed this so damn much," Jonathan whispered with a worshipful breath. He reached up and closed his hands over her breasts, massaging the tender flesh once again. Ivana flattened her palms over his pecs and began to pump her hips, lifting herself nearly all the way off his cock before planting herself on it again. They moved with a slow, even rhythm, reveling in each other. After a few minutes she began to pick up the pace, twisting her hips slightly on the way down.

He was so close to losing it. Too damn close. He wanted this to last for hours—for days. He never wanted it to end.

But his fevered body could only take so much before it had to find release. Clamping his hands on her waist, Jonathan held her steady while he pumped his hips up, moving in rapid succession, his legs straining with the need to move faster and faster until, finally, he exploded with an orgasm so strong it nearly took him out.

Ivana rode his erection for another few seconds before her inner walls clenched around him. She called out his name, her legs shaking. Jonathan ran his hands up and down her firm thighs, then up to her flat stomach. He lifted his head and licked both nipples again, still unable to get enough of her.

"Have you any idea how much I needed that?" she said with a breathless laugh.

"If it's anywhere near how much I needed it, yeah, I think I know how you feel right now."

She looked down at him, an angel with wild hair and flushed skin. She leaned over and kissed him. It was slow and deep and erotic enough to make his dick twitch with excitement, despite what had just happened a few minutes ago.

"I can never have enough of you," she said. "Even after all this time, there's nothing that compares to you."

So many thoughts swirled around in his head, but all Jonathan could think about was allowing his body a few minutes to rest so they could do this again and again and again. Now that he had her in this bed, he didn't want to let her go. Ever.

Chapter Ten

"I CAN'T BELIEVE I let you do this," Ivana said from the passenger seat.

"You don't trust me?" Jonathan asked, a humorous lilt to his voice.

"The fact that I *do* trust you is the only reason I allowed you to put this blindfold over my eyes. But if I don't take it off soon I'm going to start to hyperventilate."

"We're almost there," he said. "I promise, it'll be worth it."

She sucked in a slow breath and tried to calm herself, despite the needles of anxiety prickling her skin. She'd spent the past week trusting her body and her heart to him, what were a few more minutes at the mercy of this blindfold?

Just thinking about this past week sent a current of desire shooting through Ivana's veins. It was exactly what she'd feared would happen if she found herself back in Jonathan's arms. She now couldn't stomach the thought of ever leaving them.

And she hadn't. They'd been together every single night

this week, but always at her place. It had taken great effort for her not to think of the many women he'd been with over these past three years, but she knew she wouldn't be able to ignore it if she spent the night in the same bed where he'd made love to them.

The subject of past relationships had yet to come up. Not that she was complaining. If Jonathan asked, she would have to tell him about her time with Xander Robinson, and Ivana still wasn't sure how to do that.

They'd dated for less than two months, and the entire time she and Xander were together, she'd felt as if she was cheating on Jonathan. It was foolish. She hadn't so much as even thought about being with another man until nearly a year after she'd left New Orleans, and when she finally did come to terms with the fact that she needed to move on, she'd been blessed to find someone as kind and patient as Xander, a Haitian doctor who had worked with their relief group.

But her heart had never been in it. The first time she'd allowed Xander to spend the night, she'd awakened the next morning drowning in guilt. That's when Ivana knew she was pretty much done for when it came to men. Her strong feminist spirit had railed against the thought of being forever ruined for all but one man, but her heart wouldn't allow her to lie to herself.

And here she was again, back with the one man she craved like no other.

What if she told him right here, right now that she wasn't going back to Haiti? That she planned to stay? Would he be willing to give their love a second chance?

Ivana knew he still didn't trust her, and that, despite his claim to the contrary, he hadn't truly forgiven her for what she'd done to him three years ago. If that was the case, he wouldn't have suggested this "let's pretend everything is fine for the next few weeks" farce they were now engaged in. He would have been opened to hashing things out, instead of evading the hard conversation they *must* have in order to truly move forward.

What if she forced him to listen? Would he understand why she left? If she told him about the suffocating fear that had been eating away at her in the weeks leading up to their wedding, how flashbacks of her marriage to Michael had consumed her? Would he be able to truly forgive her then?

She wasn't sure she was ready for that answer either. Instead, she would be satisfied with where she now found herself, back in Jonathan's good graces. She may not ever earn his complete forgiveness, but at least she was no longer the target of his scorn.

The car pulled to a stop and the engine powered off.

"Okay," Jonathan said. Ivana waited while he untied the knot at the back of her head. "We're here."

The fabric fell from her eyes and Ivana's eyes widened.

"Oh, my goodness," she breathed, taking in the familiar building with the welcoming red door and hand-painted sign above it proclaiming it as Ethel's House.

Ivana's heart melted in a thick puddle around her feet. Years ago, when she'd finally agreed to go out on a date with him, she'd brought Jonathan here to Ethel's House, a food pantry that served meals to the homeless. He'd been frustrated at her reluctance to let him wine and dine her, but he'd rolled up his sleeves and didn't stop until every hungry soul was fed. She'd started falling in love with him that very night.

"Let's go," Jonathan said. "You know the people who eat here don't like to be kept waiting."

When they entered the building, Ivana was greeted by a

sea of familiar faces. Many of the volunteers she'd worked with for years were still here, still giving their all to the community around them. Several of her sisters from the voodoo religion were also at Ethel's, which didn't surprise her at all.

What *did* surprise her was Jonathan's camaraderie with everyone. Ivana's mouth gaped as he went from person to person, sharing hugs and apologizing for not being around these last few months. When he came to stand next to her again, she peered at him with a curious frown.

"Have you been volunteering here all the while I've been gone?" she asked.

"I'll explain later," he said. "Right now we've got some spaghetti and meatballs to dish out."

They made their way into the open hall, where two dozen tables were filled with people of all ages and races. Seeing the little ones always tore at Ivana's heart.

A line instantly formed the moment Bettina Simmons, Ethel Simmons's granddaughter and the long-time director of the food pantry, announced they were ready to serve dinner. After an hour of handing out chocolate pudding cups, Jonathan guided Ivana to the kitchen, where another set of workers—most who were unfamiliar to her—were packing to-go boxes.

"Bettina was able to secure a grant last year from a private philanthropic group," Jonathan explained. "Not only are they able to feed the folks here three times a week, but they also send them home with a plate and a small bag of groceries."

"You and that modesty," came Bettina's voice. She joined them, giving Jonathan's arm a playful slap. "The way he tells it, you'd think he had nothing to do with it. We got that grant because *he* went out looking for it, and *he* secured it for us."

"I helped," Jonathan said, a self-deprecating smile curling up one side of his mouth.

"Helped." Bettina rolled her eyes. She patted Jonathan's shoulder and gave Ivana a kiss on the cheek. "It's great to see you again. Don't be a stranger. You two go grab something to eat."

"Yes, ma'am." Jonathan saluted her.

He motioned for Ivana to precede him to the counter, where they fixed themselves plates of spaghetti and meatballs, green salad, buttered corn and garlic bread. They carried their plates, along with cans of soda, to a table in the corner of the hall.

Once they were seated, Ivana said, "So you *did* continue to work here."

"Actually, it took me a while to come back," he admitted with a shrug. He cut into a meatball, but then set down his fork and brought his elbows up on the table. He rubbed his hands together as if trying to warm them. "It wasn't easy to face this place after you left. I just despised being near anything that reminded me of you."

His words, though spoken softly, cut across her face like a whip.

"That's...understandable," Ivana said.

"No, Ivana. You don't understand." He released a heavy breath. "For a while there, I wouldn't let anyone even mention you when they were around me. Your name was like poison. And even though I'd come to love the charity work we used to do together, I just couldn't continue doing it."

He picked up the fork, but again set it down without taking a bite.

"About a year ago—maybe a little less than that—a friend came to visit me. She told me about this mentorship program she was involved with at her old firm. Seeing the way her eyes lit up as she described it triggered something in me. I recognized that gleam. I used to have the same look in mine when I was out here, helping out the community."

He lowered his head briefly, then looked up at her again, a measure of gratitude in his compelling gaze.

"You brought out the best in me, Ivana. You made me a better man—a better human being." He hunched his shoulders. "I decided it was time I come back to Ethel's, and Bettina and the crew welcomed me with open arms."

"I'm sure they did," she said. "They're always happy for any bit of help they can get. Was your friend's visit also the reason you started mentoring Nicolas?"

He nodded. "Well, the reason I started mentoring in general. I went through several law students before Nicolas. The first kid quit after the first week. Not just the mentorship program, but everything. Dropped out of law school completely. I began to wonder if the mentoring was really something I wanted to do."

"Ouch." Ivana grimaced. "Was it something you said?" she asked, only half joking.

"Actually, it *was* something I said. He came to me after he quit to thank me. He'd wanted to be a science fiction novelist from the time he was a kid, but his parents pushed him to go to law school. The very first conversation I had with him was about the pressures of the profession. I told him that he really had to have a passion for it if he wanted to succeed as a lawyer." He shrugged. "Guess he didn't have the passion for it."

"He was lucky to have landed you as a mentor. Imagine how miserable he'd be if he'd gone through four years of law school, knowing his heart wasn't in it," Ivana said. "I've been there before. I deeply regret the years I spent in that soul-sucking job."

"Are you happy now?" Jonathan asked after several moments passed. His voice was soft. Nearly a whisper. "Have you found your life's passion working in Haiti?"

This was her chance. She could tell him right now that she very likely was not going back. But this wasn't where she wanted to share that news. She would wait until they were alone, and not surrounded by dozens of strangers.

"It's probably the most fulfilling thing I've ever been a part of," Ivana said. "The poverty is devastating, yet there's so much joy. We go into schools to help the medical professionals provide immunizations and the kids are just so happy, despite the little they have. It's been life-changing."

His smile was brief, rueful. "Pretty hard to compete with that."

The lump that formed in her throat made it hard to swallow. She reached over and captured his hands.

"There's no competition between the two, Jonathan. I'm grateful for the experience I've had with Operation: Heal. But what I had with you..." She paused. Swallowed. Debated the wisdom of putting herself out there, and decided that if she didn't go for what she wanted right now, she might never get it. "What I pray nightly that I can have with you again," she continued. "That also was life-changing."

His eyes fell shut and he expelled a heavy breath.

"Don't do this to me." He opened his eyes. "We've been through this already. I'm not going to let you hurt me again, Ivana."

"I won't," she said.

He extracted his hands from her hold.

"This week has been...it's been like something out of a dream. I wasn't sure I'd ever see you again, so to spend this time with you—to kiss you again—it's been amazing. But if your plan is to somehow make me forget what you put me through, it's not going to happen. Can you stick to what we agreed, or should we just end this now?"

She feared her voice would crack if she tried to speak, but she knew she had to make things clear. "No, I don't want to end it," she said.

"Do you understand where I'm coming from?" he asked. "Why I'm so damn afraid to trust this—to trust you?"

She nodded. "I do," she said.

"Do you know what scares me the most in all of this? I came so close to saying yes a minute ago," he said. He closed his eyes again. "Sometimes I think the easiest thing in the world would be to just forget about these past three years and go back to allowing myself to love you again." He looked at her. "But then I think about how I'll feel when you leave in a few weeks and I just know that I can't do that."

This time he was the one who reached for her hand. He brought her fingers to his lips and pressed a gentle kiss on them, and her heart felt as if it would burst with the longing that filled it.

"I'm always going to love you, Ivana. But letting myself fall back *in* love with you—it's more than just misguided, it borders on insane. It's setting myself up for heartache."

"I know all too well about heartache," she whispered. "I don't want to cause you any more than I already have. Let's just continue the way we've been going."

He dropped his head and gave her fingers a gentle squeeze. "Thank you," he said. When he lifted his head, the smile on his lips was one of relief. "Our time together may not be long, but I promise to make it count." He winked. "I can't wait to show you what I have planned for you next."

JONATHAN STOOD off to the side, observing Ivana as she methodically studied every ruffle and button on the green and white gown, her eyes filled with wonder. When he'd read about the exhibit of gowns and other items from England's Regency period at a small museum in West Feliciana Parish, Jonathan knew he had to bring her here.

Witnessing the joy on her face as she examined each piece with such awe made the two-hour Friday afternoon road trip more than worth it. He was hard-pressed not to fall completely back in love with her.

He couldn't help the rueful grin that tilted up the corner of his lips. As if he'd ever fallen out of love with her. No matter how much he tried to pretend he'd shut her out of his life completely, she'd always been there. Thoughts of her lingered, lying dormant in the recesses of his mind, waiting patiently for something to trigger them. Seeing her like this was triggering as hell.

"Do you see this craftsmanship?" Ivana asked, pointing to the delicate lace covering the bust of a powder-blue gown. "It's amazing, isn't it?"

"Amazing," Jonathan agreed with a nod, although he hadn't paid much attention to any of the items on exhibit. His sole focus had been on her.

There wasn't much on display; only six gowns, little purses that she'd informed him were called reticules, a few fancy, silver hair combs, parasols, and a couple of perfume bottles. He feared she would be disappointed that they'd come all this way for such a small exhibit, but if the look on her face was any indication, he'd hit it out of the park.

She turned to him, the glimmer in her eyes confirming that he had indeed done exceptionally well with this little outing.

Little did she know, there was still so much more to come.

"Thank you so much for this," Ivana said as she returned to his side. "I know this isn't really your thing."

"With the amount I'm investing in this new club that's based on all this Regency era stuff, I'd better make it my thing."

As the sound of her musical laugh wrapped itself around him, Jonathan knew he would be left to figuring out a way to pick up the pieces of his twice-broken heart when she went back to Haiti. He'd known it when he made that proposition. Every second she remained in his presence solidified the fact that he was doomed to never get over her.

He loved this woman. He would always love her.

"There's more to come," he said, taking her by the hand and lacing their fingers together.

"I'm not sure what you have planned, but I can promise you it won't top this. This is the pinnacle for me."

His brow arched. "You sure about that?"

She pulled her bottom lip between her teeth, her brown cheeks reddening. "Okay, so there may be a couple of ways you can top it."

His head flew back with his laugh. "Come on, according to the map I pulled up on my phone, the next stop is only a five minute walk."

They left the small museum and continued on a short pathway that brought them to a cottage with a thatched roof. Jonathan could admit to being charmed by the replication of a quaint English village.

When they entered the cottage, Ivana gasped.

Yes. Just the reaction he was hoping for.

The whimsical English tea room was filled with the kind of furniture Jonathan was afraid he'd break just by touching it with his pinky finger. Lace tablecloths adorned the small round tables and the dainty wooden chairs each had a satin sash tied around the spindled back. Each was set with satin placemats that matched the chair sashes and flower-patterned china cups and saucers.

"This is absolutely darling," Ivana said. "I had no idea this place existed."

"There wasn't enough time for a trip back to London. This seemed like the next best thing."

Her eyes gleamed with her warm smile. "You truly are the sweetest man I've ever known," she said.

"Well, hello." A short, plump woman who looked as if she was born with the sole purpose of running an English teahouse came from behind a wall lined with shelves of tea cups in various patterns. "You must be the Campbell party," she said, extending her hand. "I'm JoAnne, the owner of A Perfect Cup. Welcome."

"I'm Jonathan and this is Ivana," Jonathan said, shaking her hand. "Thank you for taking us at the last minute."

"Oh, it was no problem at all. I've been looking forward to hosting you ever since you mentioned you were bringing someone who truly appreciates a proper English tea. Come in, come in." She made a flourishing gesture toward the table next to a window. "I thought the view of the garden would be nice for you today. There are many more blooms in the spring, but it's still a charming view, in my opinion."

"It's lovely," Ivana said as she sat.

"We have over one hundred flavors," JoAnne proudly announced as she handed them menus. "Look these over and I will take your orders the moment I return."

Since moving to the South his tea choices had consisted of sweet, extra sweet and super sweet, so Jonathan figured he was in for something pretty spectacular. He observed Ivana over the top of his menu and mentally high-fived himself. At one time, he lived to put that smile on her face. He now realized it was for his benefit as much as for hers.

JoAnn returned with a three-tiered serving platter covered with tiny, crustless sandwiches, chocolate-covered strawberries, and an assortment of miniature desserts. After Ivana revealed that she'd just visited the Regency era exhibit, their hostess took the liberty of joining them at the table and consuming every minute of their tea time.

Jonathan made several attempts to join in the conversation, but gave up after offering his opinion on the one Jane Austen adaptation he happened to catch while channel surfing and being told he was wrong, wrong, wrong. He made a mental note to look up Colin Firth on the IMDB, then sat back and enjoyed watching Ivana and her new friend delight in all things Regency England.

"Okay," she said, once JoAnn finally cleared their table. "This was close to topping the exhibit. Not quite there, but pretty close."

"Really," Jonathan said. "Do I get another try?"

"What else could you possibly do to top this?"

A half hour later, he earned yet another stellar reaction from her as they rounded a curve and The Saint Francisville Inn came into view. The newly-restored nineteenth century Victorian inn sat nestled under a collection of towering, moss-laden oak trees, and was even more beautiful than it had appeared online.

Jonathan grabbed the overnight bag he'd packed before leaving from the trunk.

"You certainly thought of everything, didn't you?" Ivana said with a laugh. "Not that I'm surprised. When you decide to do something, you never go halfway."

"And I'm not about to start," he said, placing a quick kiss on her lips.

They walked up the stairs to the wraparound porch and, when they entered the house, were greeted with flutes of complimentary champagne. The owner offered a tour of the house and grounds, which Ivana eagerly agreed to. The courtyard and pool were impressive, and Jonathan could see them enjoying drinks in the wine parlor later, but right now all he could think about was getting her alone.

By the time they were given keys and directions to The Azalea Room—their room—he was wound so tight Jonathan knew he'd have to take some time to calm himself down.

Ivana was having none of that.

The minute they entered the room, she closed the door and backed him up against it.

"You win," she said. "This tops everything."

She cupped his face in her hands and brought his mouth to hers, opening her lips and receiving his tongue as if it were a treasured gift. Her hands went to his waistband, grabbing at his shirt. Then she went after his belt buckle and the fly of his pants.

As she helped him out of his clothes, Jonathan returned the favor, dropping the overnight bag at their feet and peeling her sweater and dress from her body. Kissing like a couple of horny teenagers on prom night, they stumbled over to the king size bed. They were too hot for each other to bother with the bedding; going at it on top of the white duvet.

Jonathan kissed his way up and down her torso, lapping his tongue around her small, perfect breasts and sucking her nipple into his mouth. She tasted of the rose-scented talc she dusted over her chest when getting dressed in the morning. He reveled in her flavor, his hunger level spiking with each delicious lick.

He'd intended for the foreplay to last longer, but the moment Ivana reached down and closed her warm palm around his erection, he only had one goal in mind. Jonathan shoved himself off the bed and retrieved a condom from the carry-on bag, rolling it on before he made it back to the bed.

She waited for him with her long, glorious legs slightly open, a tantalizing invitation to heaven on earth. A low, animalistic groan climbed from his throat as he settled between her thighs, entering her with one smooth motion.

Heaven. Pure, soul-cleansing, mind-numbing pleasure enveloped his entire being. Nothing in this world could ever compare to the sensation that came over him the moment he slipped into her welcoming warmth.

"You are divine," Jonathan whispered in her ear as he plunged deep, sinking into her heat, relishing the hot, snug fit of her body around his. His heart thumped erratically within his chest as they found an intoxicating rhythm, her hips lifting to meet him thrust for thrust.

Jonathan tried with everything within him to stave off the climax that began to build at the small of his back, but he had a better chance of fending off a lion with his bare hands. He brought his thumb to his mouth and coated it before reaching between their bodies and stroking her clit.

Ivana went off like cannon fire, her body vibrating beneath him, catapulting him straight into the strongest, most electrifying climax he'd experienced in years. He surrendered his all, glorying in the sensations shooting through his bloodstream.

He collapsed on top of her, then quickly rolled off, wrapping her in his arms and pulling her in close. He pressed dozens of tender kisses along her hairline, down her jaw, behind her ear. He couldn't get enough of her.

Would there ever be a time when she didn't own him completely, body and soul? He could deny it until his grave, but Jonathan knew in his heart of hearts that he was forever hers. There wasn't a soul on this earth he could ever love as profoundly as he loved her.

"Why, Ivana?" Jonathan asked, his voice a harsh whisper.

He'd avoided asking this question for the last few weeks, having convinced himself that it was better not to bring it up. But as he looked upon her flushed face, replete with satisfaction, he *needed* to know why she left. Why, when *this* could have been their life together, had she taken off, leaving him with nothing but heartache and memories?

"We had so many plans. We were so damn perfect together. What made you leave?"

She stared into his eyes, hers filled with remorse. "I was scared," she said.

He'd expected that answer, but he wouldn't allow her to get away with it. Being afraid wasn't a good enough reason to leave him without a word and stay away for three long years.

"That's bullshit," he said. "What did you have to fear? What had I done to make you so afraid that your only way out was to leave the fucking country, Ivana?"

She put a hand to his chest.

"I know it doesn't sound like much of an excuse, but try to look at it from my perspective. I spent years in a marriage that made me miserable. I spent years in a career that made me just as miserable. And why? Because I was told it's what I *should* have wanted. I didn't find myself—my *true* self—until I left both the career and my ex-husband.

"I was free. For years, I happily lived in my own truth, with no one else defining me, no job giving me my self-worth." She brought her hand up from his chest and rested her palm against his cheek. "Then you walked into my world and changed everything."

"I never tried to change you, Ivana. Why would I ever *want* to change you? I fell in love with that gorgeous woman who was courageous enough to live in her own truth."

"I know," she said. "But the fear was still there, and the closer it got to the wedding, the more it built up, until I thought it would suffocate me. I was afraid that once I became Mrs. Jonathan Campbell, I would stop being Ivana Culpepper. And I...I panicked. That's the only way to describe it."

She dipped her head, her voice growing soft. "When I got a call from a friend I hadn't seen in years, telling me about the relief effort in Haiti, I saw it as a way to escape. I never meant to stay away as long as I did," she said. "I thought I would go there, clear my head, make sure I was really ready to become your bride, and then I'd return home. But it wasn't that easy."

"You didn't even call, Ivana. Not a single email, or text, or anything. You were my life, and you just left me without a word."

"I was ashamed," she whispered. "I know it's not an excuse, but it's the truth."

Jonathan closed his eyes and released a slow breath.

"How can I ever trust you again? How do I know you won't pull something like this in the future?" He shook his head. "Not that it matters. You're leaving in a few weeks anyway."

"I—" she started, but then she stopped. "I'm sorry," she said. "I know you said you don't want to hear it anymore, but it feels as if I can't say it enough." She caressed his jaw with her thumb, stroking back and forth. "No matter where I am in this world, I promise to never shut you out again."

She took his hand, pressed a kiss to the center of his palm, and placed it in the center of her chest.

"This is where I carry you. Always."

There was no longer any doubt in his mind that heartache lay just around the corner. But then he'd known from the moment she showed up on his doorstep that it would break his heart to see her leave yet again. No matter where she was in the world, she was destined to be his greatest source of joy, and his greatest source of anguish.

And he was destined to love her through it all.

Chapter Eleven

A SLOW, satisfied smile spread across Ivana's lips as the sun's warmth crept along her bare skin. It had been so long since she'd felt this satiated. This replete.

Her earlier aversion to spending the night in Jonathan's bed now seemed silly. The knowledge that there had been others that lay here with him in the years she'd been away didn't change the fact that *she* was here now. That she *belonged* here. As much as she'd enjoyed their night at The Saint Francisville Inn, Ivana was actually grateful that they couldn't extend their stay for the entire weekend. She wanted to be in *this* bed. *His* bed.

She stretched her legs out, then wrapped them around his waist. Her grin grew just a bit more wicked as she felt the muscle between his legs began to pulse, even as his light snores continued to sound throughout the quiet room. She pressed a kiss to his bare chest and lay her head against it, but then laughed when his hand found its way to her backside and squeezed.

She looked up at him. "I thought you were still sleeping."

"So did I. Another part of me, however, is very much awake." He twisted his hips just a bit, bringing his hardening erection in contact with her inner thigh.

Ivana reached between them and wrapped her hand around it. She slowly began to massage him, sliding her palm up and down his stiffening cock and squeezing gently. Jonathan lifted his hips up as he pressed the back of his head into the pillow, thrusting into her hand.

Watching the scene play out as it had so many times in the past, it felt as if she was living in a fantasy. It wasn't long before he was rigid and ready for her. Ivana climbed onto his lap and guided him inside, her core stretching deliciously around him. She wouldn't have thought her body could take any more of this after the night they'd shared, but the body was an amazing thing when it came to pleasure. The more it received, the more it wanted. And when it came to pleasuring her, no one could do it quite like Jonathan.

He took her to heights she hadn't reached in far too long, turning her onto her back and driving himself deeper and deeper, until a powerful orgasm swept through her body. Ivana fell back onto the bed in a heap of exhausted, satisfied woman. She'd been addicted to him from the very first time she made love with him, and that addiction had come roaring back with a vengeance. Now that she had him in her life again, she couldn't help but imagine spending countless mornings like this, in bed with the man she loved.

"Why don't you stay here with me?" he asked in a hushed voice.

Her eyes canvassed his face as she tried to interpret whether or not she'd heard him correctly.

"What do you mean?" Ivana asked.

"Exactly what I just said." He brought his hand up to

the back of her neck and kneaded it with his fingers. "You'll be back in Haiti soon. I want you to spend what time you do have left here with me."

"But I...I just moved my stuff into my grandmother's old house," she said.

"Which took all of a few hours," he said with a deep chuckle, laying waste to her lame, hastily concocted excuse. "I'm willing to sacrifice a few more hours to move you from that house to this one, if it means waking up like this for the next few weeks."

He pressed a kiss to the spot between her ear and shoulder. "Stay with me, Ivana."

Should she tell him she wasn't returning to Haiti?

She'd responded to Patience Edwards's email just last night, while waiting for Jonathan to return with po'boys from a late-night dive bar in the French Quarter. She'd thanked Patience for the years of friendship and support, and explained that she planned to take her advice and move back to the States.

She hadn't decided whether she would return to New Orleans, because the thought of living here and not being with Jonathan was too painful to bear. But if he wanted her to spend these next few weeks with him, could it possibly mean that he would ask her to stay with him, permanently?

"Okay," she finally answered.

"Okay? Meaning we can move your things here?"

Ivana pulled her bottom lip between her teeth and nodded. "Yes. I would like that very, very much." She wrapped her arms around his neck and pulled him more firmly on top of her. "Almost as much as I'd like this," she said before she kissed him again.

They remained in bed for another hour, racking up orgasm after orgasm, until Ivana was sure she'd run out of the ability to climax. But then Jonathan buried his head between her thighs and proved her wrong.

It was after orgasm number five—or was that six?—that he rolled onto his back and, with a voice dripping with regret, explained that he needed to be in the office by ten a.m.

"On a Sunday?" Ivana complained.

"I promised Harrison that I would help him hammer out the last minute summaries for the case he's presenting before Judge Reynolds tomorrow. It shouldn't take more than two, three hours, tops." He took her hand and placed a kiss in the center of her palm. "You can join us."

"I enjoy working at your law practice, but not on a Sunday," she said. "Sienna's been asking me to join her for brunch. I'll call and see if she's up for it."

They climbed out of bed and showered together, managing to get through it without tackling each other. Though, for Ivana, the temptation to pin Jonathan's naked body against the shower's stone wall and have her way with him was hard to fight.

She was forced to put on the dress she'd worn to St. Francisville on Friday. It would be wonderful when all of her things were here. Now that she'd made the decision to move in with him, she was eager for it to happen.

She borrowed Jonathan's old Mercedes, which he kept as a backup car, and drove to her Granny Elise's house to change into fresh clothes, then made the five minute drive to Satsuma Cafe to meet Sienna for brunch. Her sister was already there by the time Ivana made it to the back patio abounding with large, leafy plants and tables shaded by a huge oak tree.

"Thanks for getting me out of that house," her sister

greeted, setting her drink down and standing to give Ivana a hug.

The minute they sat, Sienna narrowed her eyes and leaned forward, peering at Ivana as if she were a foreign specimen under a microscope.

"Why do you look like someone who just had morning sex?" Her sister's accusatory voice would have been funny if it weren't so annoying.

Ivana rolled her eyes. "Can you please not?"

Sienna gasped, her eyes and mouth both widening with delight. "You've been with Jonathan, haven't you?"

"Is there someone who can take my drink order?" Ivana asked, looking around and signaling for a table attendant.

"Don't try to change the subject?"

"It would be nice if I can order my food before you start to grill me," she said.

The waiter arrived and Ivana ordered a curried chicken salad wrap, along with a glass of freshly-squeezed watermelon lemonade.

The waiter hadn't made it out of earshot before Sienna said, "Okay, spill it. And when I say *it*, I mean *all* of it. "

"What do you want me to say? Yes, I've seen Jonathan, okay?"

"I know you've *seen* him. You've been working alongside him every day for the past few weeks. I want to know what else the two of you have been doing," her sister prodded, plopping her elbow on the table and propping her chin in her hand. "Give me details. All of them."

"You're not going to get *all* the details, so you can forget about that," Ivana said, her cheeks heating under Sienna's scrutiny.

"I knew it!" her sister screeched. "Y'all did it!"

"Okay, fine," Ivana hissed. She looked around,

making sure Sienna's enthusiasm hadn't garnered any stares. "Yes, Jonathan and I have been sleeping together," she said. Goodness, she knew her cheeks must be red as a fire engine. "We're going to move my things from Granny Elise's place later today. He asked me to stay with him."

Sienna's eyes bucked. "Oh, my goodness. Is this for real?"

Ivana pulled her bottom lip between her teeth. "I think so," she said with a nod. "It feels real."

"Oh, Vonnie, I'm so happy for you. For *both* of you." She started to reach over for a hug, but then pulled back. "Wait."

"What?" Ivana asked.

Sienna released a deep breath and flattened her palms on the table. "Okay, you know I'm on your side. Always. But I need you to be one hundred percent real with me. Are you going to flake out and pull another bullshit disappearing act again?"

Ivana flinched.

"You know I love you and I defended you even when you probably didn't deserve it. But I hate what you did to Jonathan. And if you do it again, I'm not going to make excuses for you this time, Vonnie."

"I don't expect you to," Ivana said, surprised she could speak past the pain in her throat. "You should know better than to think I'd ever hurt Jonathan again."

"What about when you leave?" Sienna asked. "You're sleeping with him, moving into his place? Do you really think he's going to be okay once you go back to your relief work?"

She could share her news with Sienna; divulge her plans not to return to Haiti. But she didn't want to tell anyone before telling Jonathan. He should be the first to hear it. She owed him that much.

"I will handle all of that when the time comes," Ivana said. She reached across the table and took her sister's hand. "I am *not* going to hurt him, Cee Cee. Trust me."

She'd never questioned Sienna's loyalty, but the look in her sister's eyes revealed just how much her support over the last three years was based on that loyalty, and not on approval of Ivana's actions. It was more than apparent that if she pulled another cowardly disappearing act, she would lose her one true ally.

There was no chance of that happening.

Ivana was no longer considering moving to another city. She wanted to be here with her family. She wanted to be home.

And this time she was here to stay.

THE GRAND BALLROOM at the Omni Royal Orleans Hotel was awash in green and gold silk bunting, Mackenna Arnold's campaign colors. Large projection screens flanked either side of the dais that had been set up toward the rear wall. Towering balloon columns in green, gold, and white, with *Mackenna Arnold for Mayor* signs at the very top of them, were positioned throughout the room.

The jovial mood coasting throughout the crowded space was contagious, giving Jonathan no choice but to share in the excitement. Mack had led in the polls from the very beginning of the mayoral race, but as the various precincts reported in, even the pundits were astounded by the size of the landslide victory taking place before their very eyes.

New Orleans would have a black woman as its mayor, and Jonathan couldn't be happier.

Well, actually, he *could* be happier. This past week had proven that. Nothing made him happier than going to bed with Ivana at his side and waking up to find her still there. Even the knowledge of her imminent departure couldn't squelch his joy.

Because she would return. She hadn't said it, but Jonathan felt it. He wasn't sure how long it would take, but she couldn't perform relief work forever. When the time came for her to hang up her hat, he would be here to welcome her back. Permanently.

He could wait until she was ready to leave Haiti. He had no choice; it was either wait or live without her, and he'd decided there was no living without her anymore.

Standing next to her right now, Jonathan wrapped one arm around her waist and gave her a squeeze.

"Do you think your smile can get any wider?" he asked.

"I doubt it," she said with a laugh. "I am just so incredibly happy for this city. The people here are *so* lucky to have Mackenna Arnold to lead them into the future."

"She's going to be amazing," Jonathan said. He paused for a moment before adding, "Maybe you should think about sticking around so you can witness Mack's marvelousness firsthand?"

Her eyes glittered with mischief as she swung around to fully face him. "Funny you should say that." She clasped her hands at the back of his neck. "I—"

"Ivana?"

They both turned, looking toward where someone had called her name. A woman who was almost as tall as Ivana, with a closely-shaved head and huge hoop earrings dangling from her lobes, came up to them.

"Massey!" Ivana disengaged from her embrace with Jonathan and enveloped the woman in a hug.

"I wondered if I would see you here." She returned Ivana's hug. "How are you adjusting to being back home?"

"It's been lovely," Ivana said. "It's so good to see you! How are you?"

"Relieved," the older woman said. "As I'm sure everyone else is now that Ms. Arnold will officially be this city's next mayor. I feel more comfortable with my daughter starting college here in the fall."

"Amen to that!" Ivana said. She turned to Jonathan. "Massey, this is Jonathan Campbell. Jonathan, this is Massey Jean-Julien. Massey launched a leadership academy for young girls in a small communal section of Port-Au-Prince."

"And Ivana here has been one of our most ardent supporters." She took both of Ivana's hands in hers. "I was surprised when Patience told me she finally convinced you to leave the island. I'm sorry to see you go, but you've put in your time, and then some. You'll be missed, but I understand. No one can do that work forever."

"No. Umm...it does take a toll," Ivana replied.

Jonathan wasn't sure what to make of the panic in her eyes. "No need to miss her too much. She'll be back in Haiti soon enough," he said.

The woman looked to Ivana, a mask of befuddlement clouding her features. "You're going back to Operation: Heal? I spoke with Patience just yesterday. She said you'd decided not to return."

Jonathan went completely still.

"Let's not get into that right now," Ivana said. "We should be celebrating Mack's win."

As if on cue, a roar went up, practically shaking the entire ballroom.

"They've officially called it!" Massey Jean-Julien said, pumping both fists in the air.

Everyone went wild, but the thoughts swirling around in his head wouldn't allow Jonathan to join in the merriment.

Ivana wasn't going back to Haiti? She would no longer work with the relief group? When had she decided this? Was it between the time she left his bed this morning and tonight? Because if it was any time before that, she had a hell of a lot to answer for.

"Do you have something you want to tell me?" Jonathan asked her.

"Not now," she said, her teeth clenched as she smiled at the room of celebrating supporters.

"Then when, Ivana? When you leave to go...where? Help me out here." He leaned toward her. "And why in the hell am I just hearing about this? How is it that your friend here knew you weren't going back to Haiti and I didn't? When did you decide this?"

The look of guilt that flashed across her face provided the answer.

"You knew all along, didn't you? You knew you weren't going back, and you let me think..."

He couldn't even finish the statement. Just when he'd started to trust her again. Just when he thought she trusted *him* enough to be open and honest with him.

"I can't believe you, Ivana. I can't believe I fell for this shit again."

Jonathan pivoted on his heel and started walking toward the exit, swerving through the crowd of celebrating supporters. He burst through the French doors that led to the courtyard.

"Jonathan!"

He continued walking toward the far end of the hotel's courtyard, ignoring her.

"Would you please stop and listen!" Ivana called.

He stopped and abruptly spun around to face her. "Listen to what? Do you actually have an explanation worth hearing?"

"If you would give me a minute," she said.

Jonathan pulled in a calming breath. She was right; the least he could do was give her a chance to speak.

"Okay," he said. "I'm listening."

But she didn't speak. She just stood there, staring at him.

"Are you going to say something?" he asked.

She ran a fidgeting hand through her hair, then tucked several wayward strands behind her ear. "I'm trying to figure out where to start," she said.

"Why don't you start by explaining why you kept something like this from me?" Jonathan said, bracing his legs apart and folding his arms over his chest. "Was it supposed to be a surprise? Is that it?"

"In a way, yes," she said. "I was going to tell you tonight. Just moments before Massey interrupted us."

"How did she know about your plans before I did? How long have *you* known that you weren't going back?"

Her shoulders curled forward as she wrapped her arms around her chest, clutching her elbows.

"I've been going back and forth about it for a few weeks," she finally answered.

"Weeks? And you didn't think to mention it to me? Ivana, do you know the kind of emotional rollercoaster I've been on, trying to convince myself that I'll be okay when you leave me again? Why would you let me go on believing that you were going back to Haiti at the end of this little sabbatical you're supposedly on?"

She held her hands out. "Because I wasn't sure I was going to remain in New Orleans," she said.

Jonathan's head snapped back.

"I've been pretty certain that I wasn't going to return to Haiti, or to any of Operation: Heal's relief efforts, but I hadn't made a decision about exactly where I would go."

"Where else *would* you live if not here?"

She hunched her shoulders. "I don't know. I mulled over a number of places: Houston, Atlanta, even Baton Rouge."

"An hour away? You're actually considering moving just an hour away from here? And what? Were you going to just let me think that you were still living in another country? Was that your plan?"

"Jonathan, a month ago you could barely stand to be around me. As of just a couple of weeks ago I was nothing but a temporary employee at your law firm," she said. "I was still debating whether or not I could move back to New Orleans because I was unsure if I could stomach living here if we weren't together. Do you know how heartbreaking it would be for me to live here and have to see you with other women?"

"So *now* we're worried about breaking hearts?" he said with a bitter laugh. "Yeah, I think I understand pretty well what it's like to have your heart broken. You give good lessons on that."

She closed her eyes. "Jonathan," she whispered. "Please, don't do this."

He stared at her, wondering if he'd ever really known her at all.

"Why must you always hold things back from me?" he asked. "Why can't you trust me with the important things, Ivana? That's what people who supposedly care about each other do, they fucking trust each other with the important stuff!"

"I was going to tell you," she said, holding her palms out. She opened her eyes and repeated. "I was going to tell you."

Jonathan pitched his head back and cursed up at the sky.

"I'm not sure I believe you," he said. He brought his eyes back to her, his anger growing with each moment that passed. "And that's the problem. Your credibility wasn't great to begin with after the shit you pulled three years ago. Now?" He had to take a minute before he could continue. "I vowed to never put myself in the position to have you hurt me again. I guess I can only blame myself for being foolish enough to trust you."

"Jonathan, please," she whispered.

But he didn't want to hear any more. He turned and walked away.

Chapter Twelve

"SAM NESTER from the assessor's office is on line one."

Jonathan pressed the intercom button on his phone. "He's probably looking for a campaign donation for the run-off election. Can you come up with an excuse, LaKeisha?"

"That's my job," his receptionist said. "Although I've been doing it a lot more this morning. Are you sure you're okay?"

"I'm fine," Jonathan said. "I'm just not in the mood to talk to Sam right now."

Or to anybody.

Jonathan leaned back in his chair and rested his head against the headrest. He should have gone with his first mind and called in sick. For the amount of work he'd managed to do this morning, he could have stayed home. That's what Ivana had done.

The fact that he'd been caught off guard when he'd walked into the office and been informed by LaKeisha that Ivana had called to say she wouldn't be in the office today was a testament to just how quickly he'd allowed himself to forget that running this kind of disappearing act was her favorite pastime. He shouldn't have been surprised.

Yet, he *had* been surprised, because he knew how much she'd been looking forward to today. Jonathan planned to hand over the new advocacy program she'd developed to Nicolas. It had been *her* idea after Nicolas emailed last Thursday, letting Jonathan know he would be returning from his grandmother's in Mexico.

Ivana had worked countless hours last week, making sure everything was in order so that the transition would be seamless. He hadn't thought she would allow what happened between them at Mack's election night party to rob her of the joy of handing this project over to Nicolas.

But, then again, she was a coward. She was still such a damn coward.

No matter how diligently he tried, his mind could not fend off the image of her face when her friend Massey had let it slip that Ivana wasn't planning to return to her relief aid group. He wanted to believe she had been only seconds from telling him, just as she'd claimed, but how could he ever be certain of anything when it came to her?

Jonathan grimaced, shutting his eyes tight and clutching his stomach to staunch the pain Ivana had once again caused. He sucked in several long, measured breaths, slowly releasing them as he counted to ten. Why did she have to make things so damn hard? Why was it so difficult for her to give her whole self to him—to trust him?

Was this how it would be for the rest of his life? Practicing breathing exercises to work through yet another painful episode at the hands of Ivana?

He opened his eyes and stared straight ahead.

"Yes," he whispered.

It was time he accepted that this was how it would be

from now until he drew his last breath. Because he couldn't *not* love her. Jonathan understood that now. It didn't matter what she did or how much she hurt him, he was destined to love this stubborn, infuriating, enchantingly breathtaking woman forever.

And he wasn't going to let her run away this time.

He wouldn't go to her just yet; he'd give her a bit of space for the next couple of days. Knowing how easily she was spooked, Jonathan knew better than to add any extra pressure. He didn't want give her any incentive to skip town.

Although, he was fairly certain that wouldn't happen. The invitation-by-text he'd gotten from Sienna this morning guaranteed Ivana would be in town for at least the next few days. Toby had been nominated for a Producer of the Year award by some association for music agents and producers and Sienna was throwing a small gathering on Wednesday night to celebrate.

After receiving her text, Jonathan had replied, asking if she'd told Ivana about it and, if so, had her sister given her any indication she wouldn't be able to make the party. Sienna told him she hadn't given her a chance to make any excuses, pointing out the years' worth of family get-togethers she'd missed to guilt Ivana into attending.

There was a slim chance she would defy Sienna and leave, but unlike three years ago, Jonathan wasn't willing to let her stay gone this time. If she left, he was going after her. He would not allow her cowardliness to rob them of any more time together.

He would give her these next two days to work through her fears on her own. If she needed more time, then she would have to spend it with him at her side.

He pushed his chair back from the desk and grabbed his

empty coffee mug, preparing to reward his sudden resolve with a much-needed shot of caffeine. He opened the door to his office and nearly ran smack into Nicolas.

"Whoa," Jonathan said, rearing back.

"Oh, sorry!" Nicolas said, backing up several steps. "I was just coming to see you."

"Welcome back," Jonathan said, patting Nicolas's forearm. He held up the hand with the mug. "Have a seat in my office. I'm going to grab myself more coffee and then we can talk."

LaKeisha appeared out of nowhere, snatching the mug from his hand.

"I've got it." She nudged her chin toward Jonathan's office. "You two go talk."

Nicolas hitched his thumb toward LaKeisha's retreating form. In a lowered voice, he said, "I've been meaning to ask, has she always been this bossy?"

"Yes!" His receptionist yelled from the break room.

"She also has a heightened sense of hearing," Jonathan said. He gestured for Nicolas to follow him back into his office. "Come on. There are a few things I want to discuss with you."

By the time he was settled in his chair, LaKeisha was already back with his black coffee.

"How is your grandmother?" she asked, handing Nicolas a second mug of coffee.

"Thanks." He smiled. "My grandmother's doing a lot better. She was released from the hospital two days ago. The biggest problem now is keeping her out of the kitchen. She wants to cook for all of her children now that they're all home."

"Sounds like my grandmother," LaKeisha said with a

laugh. "Glad to hear she's doing okay." She squeezed Nicolas's shoulder before leaving them alone.

"Is your uncle still there?" Jonathan asked.

"Yeah, he's going to stay for a while. Thanks to Ms. Dayton, he's already been in touch with an immigration lawyer who's going to help when he's ready to come back home—back to New Orleans."

"Back *home*," Jonathan emphasized. "And I'm happy to hear Serena is on top of things, not that I'm surprised. She's a fantastic lawyer." He leaned back in his chair. "What do you think about the kind of law she practices?" Jonathan asked him.

"Immigration law?"

Jonathan nodded. "I've watched you this past month as you worked with Ivana. You seemed to have taken an interest in it. Am I mistaken?"

"Not at all," Nicolas said. "I've...I've been thinking about it a lot. I just...I don't know. When I told my family I wanted to be a lawyer, they were all excited because it meant..." He rubbed his fingers together, the international symbol for cash. "Immigration lawyers aren't known for raking in the big bucks."

Jonathan leaned forward, putting his elbows on his desk. "I won't give you any self-righteous bullshit about how everything isn't always about the money. It's important to assess the earning potential for whatever path you choose for your future. However, if you find yourself in the right situation, you may have the chance to practice the kind of law you want to practice while also making a good living."

Nicolas's forehead crinkled in confusion. "I'm not following," he said, running his palms up and down his thighs.

"Look, Nicolas, as smart as you are, you're going to have

firms coming at you from all sides, offering you the moon in order to join them. And I wouldn't blame you one bit for taking one of them up on an offer."

"But?" Nicolas asked.

"Harrison and I would really like you to join Campbell & Holmes once you've completed your studies," Jonathan said, not wanting to beat around the bush any longer. "We want to make the advocacy program you and Ivana have been working on a permanent fixture, and I can't think of anyone better to run it than you. If you're interested, that is." Jonathan put up his hands. "I know a small, two-person law firm in the Quarter doesn't have the glitz and glamour of those big firms in the high-rises on Canal Street and Poydras, but—"

"Yes," Nicolas said. "I want it. I'll take it."

A smile curved up Jonathan's lips. It was his first real smile since Saturday night.

"Well, that was easier than I thought it would be," he said. He held his hand out to him. "Welcome to the firm."

UNPINNING the skirt from the line, Ivana clipped the wooden clothespin next to the others on her sleeve and folded her favorite ankle-length skirt over her arm. She slowly twirled the circular clothesline around, freeing the last of the garments and carrying them into the house. She dropped them onto the plain, light brown wooden table that had replaced the reddish oak one that had sat in her Granny Elise's dining room for years. She began rolling her shirts into tight logs and stuffing them into the suitcase that sat open on the table.

She'd just tucked a maxi dress into the suitcase when

her hands stilled and she nearly collapsed into a nearby chair. She folded her arm over the pile of sun-fresh laundry and dropped her head onto her forearm.

What was she doing?

"You don't have to do this," she whispered. She didn't have to run away.

But how could she remain here, knowing how Jonathan must feel about her? She'd had the chance to do the right thing. She could have talked to him, told him about Patience's suggestion that she not return to Haiti for the sake of her health, and that she was seriously contemplating heeding her supervisor's warning. What would have been the harm in just sharing that small bit of information with him?

It was as if she couldn't help but screw things up when it came to the man she loved more than any other on this earth. He didn't think he could trust her to tell him the truth, and Ivana couldn't blame him one bit. At this point, she wouldn't trust herself.

But just because she'd likely messed things up beyond repair with Jonathan didn't mean she had to leave the country. She could go with her contingency plan and move to a nearby city. That way, when she had some kind of family obligation, like the party Sienna had planned for tonight, Ivana could be just a short drive away.

The ache that had resided in her chest since Saturday night began to throb.

She didn't want to leave New Orleans. This city was a part of her. It was in her bones, in her very marrow. She'd fallen in love with it all over again—had been reminded every time she passed a saxophonist blowing out a bluesy tune on a corner in the Quarter, or caught a whiff of spicy jambalaya from the open window of a nearby restaurant, just how much there was to cherish about this place of her heart.

She was startled by a knock at the front door.

"One minute," she called, certain it was yet another real estate scout coming to ask if she was interested in selling her property. She peered out the front door's small crescent-shaped window and blinked twice at the sight of Willow Holmes's smiling face staring at her from the other side.

"Hey there." Willow waved.

Ivana opened the door. "Willow! Hello!" she said with a hug. "What brings you here?"

"I was at that cute new cafe on Piety Street and took a chance that you would be here," she said, stepping inside at Ivana's urging. "I hope it's okay that I stopped by."

"Of course," Ivana said. "Can I get you something to drink?"

"No, I won't be long. I just wanted to quickly talk to you about something."

"At least sit," Ivana said. She guided her toward the couch and they both took a seat. "What's up?"

"Well, I was speaking to Sienna this morning, and she mentioned that you were home to stay. Harrison was under the impression that you were only here on a short leave and would be returning to Haiti."

"It was up in the air for a while," Ivana said.

"So, *are* you here to stay?" Willow asked.

She hesitated for a second before she answered, "Yes. Yes, I'm here to stay," Ivana said.

The relieved smiled that spread across Willow's face was both touching and a bit confusing. Ivana wouldn't have thought her plans would have mattered that much to her.

"That is so good to hear," Willow said. She folded her hands in her lap. "Now that I know you intend to remain in the city, I have a proposition for you. Wait, are you still working on that program for the firm? I think it's amazing and necessary what you've helped Harrison and Jonathan set up, by the way."

"I'm done with that," Ivana said. "Jonathan was going to ask Nicolas Flores if he would run the program."

"Oh, that's perfect. Nicolas is such a sweetheart, and so smart. I hope he accepts the offer. I'll have to ask Harrison about it when I get home." Willow clapped her hands together. "So, this may work out even better than I thought," she said. "You know about the foundation we've set up in Diane's name, correct?"

"Speaking of amazing and necessary things," Ivana said.

Willow nodded. "The response has been phenomenal. In fact, we've gotten so much press and support that we're going to need more help. Indina and I have interviewed several candidates, but the only one who had everything we were looking for in a director was just offered a position in Jacksonville that was too good to pass up. And then, like a gift from God, I find out that you're moving back to New Orleans."

Ivana's heartbeat began to escalate. "Are you asking me to run the foundation?"

"Yes," Willow said. She put her hands up. "Let me explain a few things. First, we're still in the early stages, so this isn't a full-time, forty hours a week job. I've been doing much of the work so far, and I'd say I've spent maybe four to five hours a day, so you're looking at part-time employment for the first few months. However, based on how everything has progressed since the launch, I have no doubt we'll need a full-time director soon."

"Can I ask why you don't want to stay on as the director?" Ivana asked.

"As much as I would love to stay on, I can't," Willow said with a smile that contradicted her apologetic tone. "I was just accepted into the graduate program at Tulane."

"Wow!" Ivana hugged her. "Congratulations! What are you studying?"

"Biomedical Engineering," Willow said. "That's just one reason I still plan to work closely with you. One of the foundation's goals is to offer STEM-related activities for girls, so in between classes and lab work, I plan to help develop programming for the after-school clinics and summer boot camp we want to start.

"I know this is a lot to consider, and you probably already have a job lined up, but I hope you do consider it, Ivana. The Diane Holmes Foundation needs someone who is committed to helping those who really need it, and I don't know a single person who has given more of her time to helping others than you. You're an inspiration."

Ivana's throat tightened to the point she could barely speak.

"Well, if I knew you'd make me cry I would have never let you in the house," she said.

Willow laughed, then in an almost pleading tone, asked, "Will you think about it?"

Ivana nodded. "I'll think about it. I don't want to give you an answer on the spot, but I'm 99.9% sure that I'm a yes."

Willow's eyes went wide. "Are you? Oh, Ivana. I promise not to pressure you into doing anything that isn't right for you, but I feel it in my bones that this is right. With the way everything has fallen into place with this foundation, I wouldn't be surprised if Diane isn't up there running this whole thing from heaven."

"She would be the one to do it," Ivana said with a laugh.

She sobered. "Thank you for entrusting me to lead something that's so important to the entire Holmes family—to this city. That means a lot to me."

"I hope you say yes, Ivana." She put her hands up. "No pressure! No pressure, but we would love to have you."

After gathering her in another hug, Ivana led Willow to the door and walked her out to her car. Once inside again, she went over to the open suitcase and stared at the contents. A thick, uncomfortable knot formed in her throat. She tipped her head back, closed her eyes and pulled in a deep breath.

When she opened her eyes again, she knew what she had to do. A sense of peace washed over her as she began to remove the rolled up shirts from the suitcase. She went into the bedroom and placed them in the second drawer of the cedar chest of drawers, then went back into the dining room and gathered the rest of the clothes she'd taken in from the line.

After she'd put away her clothes, Ivana rolled the suitcase into the bedroom and tucked it inside the closet. She didn't plan to take it back out anytime soon.

Maybe she would rent this house from Sienna. Or maybe she would look into buying one of her own.

Or maybe she could convince Jonathan to give her another chance.

"You have some nerve," Ivana whispered.

It was downright ballsy of her to presume Jonathan would be willing to ever see her face again, but if it took the rest of her life, Ivana was determined to earn his forgiveness.

No matter what happened, she was home to stay.

JONATHAN MADE the block around Toby's house, searching for a parking space that wouldn't result in his car being covered in a pile of leaves and acorns later tonight. Parking was a bitch in this neighborhood if you didn't make it here before the residents came home from work. He'd planned to leave the office over an hour ago, just after Harrison had, but a phone call from a client had held him up.

He managed to slip into a space in front of Toby and Sienna's next-door neighbor's house—a space that was, thankfully, free of arching oak tree branches. He walked up to the front door and rang the doorbell, scrolling through live basketball scores on the NBA's Twitter feed as he waited for someone to answer.

Jonathan had almost managed to convince himself it was the chill in the air that had his hands slightly trembling, and not nervousness over seeing Ivana when he walked into the house. Or worse, not seeing her.

She's in there.

She had to be there. Not because she wouldn't leave New Orleans without saying goodbye to him. She'd proven three years ago she had no problem doing that. But she wouldn't leave if Sienna had asked her to stay. When it came to her baby sister, Ivana was nothing if not loyal.

After a minute or so, Toby opened the front door, a broad smile stretched across his face. "My man." He held his hand out. "Thanks for coming!"

"As if I would miss this," Jonathan said, slapping his offered palm and bringing him in for a one-armed hug. "Congrats, man. I'm proud of you."

They stepped into the foyer and he clamped a hand on Toby's shoulder. "Now, when it comes to winning this Producer of the Year thing—"

"I know, I know," Toby interrupted him. "It doesn't matter if I win or lose. It's an honor just to be nominated."

"Bullshit. If you don't win I'm clowning you like a dog."

Toby barked out a laugh. "I'd do the same to you."

"I know damn well you would," Jonathan said with a grin. He followed Toby to the open-concept kitchen, living, and dining room, and did a scan of the space. He quickly swallowed the panicked feeling that threatened to come over him when he didn't spot Ivana anywhere. Maybe she was in the bathroom? Or maybe Sienna and Toby's kids were at home and she was in their room reading them a bedtime story?

"Hey honey." Sienna walked over to him, tilting her cheek up for a kiss.

Jonathan obliged, then whispered in her ear. "Is your sister around?"

Sienna's brow furrowed. "I thought she would have come over with you."

His heart skipped several beats. She wasn't here.

Don't panic.

"I was late leaving the office," Jonathan said.

There were a million and one possible explanations for Ivana's tardiness. He wouldn't jump to the worse-case scenario.

What Jonathan found most interesting was that Ivana hadn't mentioned anything to Sienna about Saturday night. If she had told her sister about their argument at Mack's victory celebration, Sienna wouldn't have assumed Ivana would have come here with him.

There were several ways to interpret that, but Jonathan was taking it as a positive. Unless she planned to send Sienna a text from whatever far off country she'd fled to.

"I'm sure she's on her way," he said, though the only

thing he knew for certain was that he would find her, wherever Ivana eventually landed. If he had to practice law from Haiti, he would do it.

He joined the party, chatting with Ezra Holmes about Mackenna's transition plans for the mayor's office now that his fiancée was officially mayor-elect for the city of New Orleans. Jonathan then moved to the array of hors d'oeuvres displayed on the marble island that delineated the start of the kitchen, but he could barely swallow the small bite of crab cake he attempted to eat. Being unsure of Ivana's whereabouts had set his nerves on edge.

Jonathan had checked his watch no fewer than a dozen times in the last half hour when the doorbell sounded and Sienna left the room to answer it. He heard a pair of muffled feminine voices coming from the foyer, but didn't release the breath he'd been holding until Sienna emerged with Ivana in tow.

Thank God.

Thank God. Thank God. Thank God.

Pretending to be calm and unbothered had taken more effort than he first anticipated.

He wouldn't pounce on her just yet. He would give her space. Maybe let her grab a bite to eat and chat with a few guests before he approached and explained to her that he was not willing to let her go so easily this time.

This time, he planned to fight for her.

But the moment Ivana entered the living room, *she* headed straight for *him*.

"Can I speak to you?" she asked, then grabbed his jacket cuff and tugged him toward the hallway that led to the bedrooms. They slipped into the Zenobia's room. She flipped on the light switch and the bright primary colors on the walls nearly blinded him.

"Ivana—" Jonathan started, but she stopped him.

"Please, let me say this before you say anything." She pulled in a deep breath and released it. "I love you. I don't deserve your love or your forgiveness or your trust, but I love you, Jonathan. I will never love any man more than I love you."

A jolt of hopefulness rushed over him even as a sense of calm cascaded through him. The sensation that his heart would burst clear out of his chest had never been stronger.

"Ivana, I—"

"Please, let me finish." She held her hands up. "I'm not running away this time. I'm staying right here, and I'm going to earn your trust and your love. I know it won't be easy. I don't deserve easy." Her open, earnest expression nearly did him in. "But it *will* happen. I am going to marry you, Jonathan Campbell, and we're going to finish what we started. I can understand if you're not ready, but know that I'm going to fight for you and eventually win you back. I love you too much not to."

Her chest rose and fell following her impassioned soliloquy.

Jonathan took a moment to study her, his eyes roaming slowly over the face of this woman he loved like his very life depended on it. She was the very breath in his lungs. And she was his. Always.

"And here I thought I would have to go chasing halfway around the world after you," he finally said.

She blinked several times, confusion clouding her face.

"What?" she asked.

Jonathan took a step toward her, then another. "When you didn't show up to the office Monday morning, I'd convinced myself that you had run away again."

"I'm sorry," she said. Her eyes fell close. "I'm so, so sorry."

"But I had every intention of going after you this time," he finished.

Her eyes flew open. "You...you did?"

He brought his hand up to her face and drew the backs of his fingers along her jaw line. "You are my world, Ivana Culpepper. You've been my world—my everything—from the moment I met you. I won't let fear keep us apart ever again. You returned to me once, but you won't get a chance to do it again because I'm not letting you slip away this time."

"I don't want to," she said. "Three years ago, I left because I was afraid becoming your wife would somehow rob me of my identity. That I would lose myself. I'm no longer afraid." She took both his hands in hers and kissed his fingers, then she flattened them against her heart. "This belongs to you. *I* belong to you. Everything I have, I freely give it to you."

She pressed her mouth to his, and murmured against his lips.

"You never have to worry about me leaving you again. I plan to be right here with you every day. Always."

Epilogue

THREE MONTHS LATER...

"WELCOME TO CAMPBELL'S."

Ivana moved aside so the group of young women who'd just walked through the doors of the club could enter. "You must be the NOLA Stars and Stogies. We have everything set up for you. Please follow Darynda." She swept her hand toward the hostess. "She will show you to the cigar lounge."

It shouldn't have come as a surprise to anyone that a spot on the guests list for tonight's official grand opening of Campbell's—months earlier than they'd first anticipated—would be the most coveted prize in New Orleans, but Ivana still found herself in awe at the crowd. The buzz preceding tonight's big event had been even more intense than when The Hard Court opened. It had to be the uniqueness of the club. There was nothing like Campbell's in the New Orleans area. Entertainment writers from as far away as Jackson, Mississippi and Mobile, Alabama had come into town to cover tonight's festivities.

Despite the vast number of people already enjoying all the club had to offer, it didn't feel crowded. Although the only thing dividing up the space were the four thick, circular brick columns that were original to the warehouse, the high ceilings and smartly designed seating areas created the illusion of privacy. As usual, Indina had done a masterful job with her interior design.

Guests seemed to be enjoying the well-stocked bar, which boasted the most expansive selection of scotch and bourbon in the South, but it was already obvious to Ivana that Campbell's cigar lounge would be its most popular feature. The private room was booked for the next six months. What she found most fascinating was the number of women's clubs that had called to reserve the space. Cigar smoking had apparently flourished among women in the years she'd been away.

"And how is my wife doing on this lovely night?"

Ivana felt her skin grow warm as Jonathan came up behind her and pressed a kiss beneath her ear.

"Your wife is charming the pants off everyone who enters this club," she said.

She felt his deep laugh rumbling against her back. He spread his fingers low over her belly. "And how is Little Jonathan doing in there?" he asked.

She grinned. Peering at him over her shoulder, she cautioned, "You do realize if you keep assuming this baby will be a boy that it pretty much guarantees that we will have a girl, don't you?"

"I don't care what we have," he said. "As long as I finally get to see you holding my baby in your arms, I'm happy." He spun her around and locked his fingers at the base of her spine. Dipping his head, he traced her lips with a gentle, barely-there caress of his own.

Ivana felt her phone vibrating in her pocket. "Hold on a sec," she said, taking out the phone. She read the text.

Stop necking with Jonathan and get your ass over here.

With a sigh, she glanced over to where Toby and Sienna congregated with the rest of the family.

"We're being summoned," Ivana said.

"Do we have to go?"

She laughed at his whine, taking him by the hand and dragging him toward the corner of the club reserved for their family and closest friends.

"Finally," Toby said, rising from the sofa. He clamped a hand on Jonathan's shoulder. "You know, when I first walked through the doors of The Hard Court all those years ago, I was blown away. I was sure you could never come up with anything that could top it. Count on you to prove me wrong."

"I've been proving you wrong ever since your ass claimed you had a better jump shot than me," Jonathan said, bringing him in for a hug.

Nearly the entire Holmes clan had joined them for the grand opening. Monica sat with her back pressed against Eli's chest, her husband's hand resting on her hip. Willow and Harrison occupied the other side of the plush loveseat, mirroring the other couple's pose. Alex and Renee, along with Indina and her husband, Griffin, sat on the opposite sofa.

"When do Mackenna and Ezra return from their honeymoon?" Ivana asked Indina.

"Tomorrow," she answered. "They met up with Brooklyn and Reid in San Diego after their comics convention ended and they're all flying home together. I think Ezra is still a bit salty that Mack didn't want a big wedding, but he'll get over it. Besides, we still have yours," Ivana said in a sing-songy voice.

"Actually..." Ivana arched a brow at Jonathan. He lifted a shoulder in a shrug.

But before Ivana could share the news, Sienna said, "They're already married."

"*What?*"

"*When?*"

"*Why didn't you say anything?*"

Ivana held up her palms to stave off their questions. "We did it last week."

After what happened the last time she planned a big, showy wedding, Ivana and Jonathan had both decided they wanted to keep it simple this time around. In a quiet ceremony with only her sister and Toby as witnesses, she and Jonathan had finally become husband and wife. Ivana thought she couldn't be happier, until the next morning, when it had occurred to her that the tenderness in her breasts and her sudden aversion to all things citrus may have been due to something more than just a quirk or fast-developing food allergy.

She'd picked up a pregnancy test and drove straight to the law practice. Even now, Ivana felt herself warming at the unadulterated excitement on Jonathan's face when she held up the stick, displaying the positive result.

Her doctor had assured her that as long as she remained in good health and kept her stress to a minimum, there was no reason she couldn't have an easy, healthy pregnancy. Jonathan had instantly turned into a doting—somewhat neurotic—father-to-be. She told herself it was adorable and not annoying.

"Well, look who's here," Jonathan said.

Ivana turned and smiled at the sight of Nicolas striding toward them, his mother and his uncle, Javier, in tow.

"Oh, Nicolas, it is so great to see you all here," she said, greeting him with a hug. "Thanks for coming."

"This is the hottest ticket in town. We wouldn't miss this for the world," he said.

Both Nicolas's mother and his uncle thanked Ivana for the work she'd put into Campbell & Holmes's new advocacy program. After introductions to the rest of the Holmeses, the trio headed for the bar.

Jonathan came up behind her and whispered in her ear, "Follow me?"

"Where?" Ivana asked.

He grasped hold of her hand and gently tugged, leaving her with no choice but to follow. He guided her toward the small opening that led to a hidden staircase. They walked up to the narrow second story landing that looked out over the crowd below. It was exactly what she'd imagined when she read her historical romances and dreamed about entering the exclusive halls of White's gentleman's club.

There were more than a dozen cozy seating areas, some larger than others, with long sofas, shorter love seats, settees and stools, all done in varying shades of deep brown, cream, and gold. Patrons enjoyed drinks and light snacks from the bar as they conversed with friends. It was an easy, relaxed atmosphere. It was perfect.

"I still can't believe I was the inspiration for all of this," Ivana said, entwining her fingers with his and leaning her head against his arm.

"I've come to realize that you're the inspiration for everything that's good in my life," Jonathan said. He kissed her forehead. "As long as I have you here beside me, there's nothing in this life that I can't do." He brushed his thumb against her cheek. "You are my everything."

She smiled up at him, took his hand and pressed a kiss to the center of his palm. "And you're mine."

Acknowledgments

A heartfelt thank you to all the readers who have accompanied me on this journey with the Holmes family all these years. It has been a pleasure to bring these characters to life. The Holmes family will remain with me forever.

A special thanks to the lovely Danielle Marie (@belle_-marie_) and Willy Goodman of Willy Goodman Photography (@willygoodmanphotography) for my amazing cover photo.

Moments in Maplesville

Visit the sexy, sultry, small southern town of Maplesville in my *Moments in Maplesville* novella series.

A Perfect Holiday Fling (*Callie & Stefan*)

A Little Bit Naughty (*Jada & Mason*)

Just A Little Taste (*Kiera & Trey*)

I Dare You (*Stefanie & Dustin*)

All You Can Handle (*Sonny & Ian*)

Any Way You Want It (*Nyree & Dale*)

Any Time You Need Me (*Aubrey & Sam*)

Be sure to look out for *The Boyfriend Project*, the first book in my brand new series from Grand Central Forever! Coming in June 2020!

Visit my BOOKS page to see my entire backlist!

About the Author

A native of south Louisiana, Farrah Rochon officially began her writing career while waiting in between classes in the student lounge at Xavier University of Louisiana. After earning her Bachelors of Science degree and a Masters of Arts from Southeastern Louisiana University, Farrah decided to pursue her lifelong dream of becoming a published novelist. She was named *Shades of Romance Magazine*'s Best New Author of 2007. Her debut novel garnered rave reviews, earning Farrah several SORMAG Readers' Choice Awards. *I'll Catch You*, the second book in her New York Sabers series for Harlequin Kimani, was a 2012 RITA ® Award finalist. Yours Forever, the third book in her Bayou Dreams series, is a 2015 RITA® Award finalist.

When she is not writing in her favorite coffee shop, Farrah spends most of her time reading her favorite romance novels, traveling the world, and seeing as many Broadway shows as possible.